TRIXIE

Yulia Konchaov

Contents

Prologue

Words fail me as I try to describe the doctor's expression as he sat on his chair with his hands clasped above the table. Anxious? Pitying? Sad? I couldn't quite figure it out, but I knew that he was going to deliver bad news.

"Rosalinda has what we call acute lymphocytic leukemia. Her immune system is basically shut down, and we need to start treatment right away."

My head was in such a whirlwind at that moment after I heard what the doctor said about my young sister. I looked at my mom and dad's forlorn and broken expressions. I couldn't believe that this was happening. Luckily, my sister wasn't in the room since the nurses had taken her out.

"I'll give you a moment alone." The doctor said then stood up and walked out the door to give us some privacy.

My parents and I were silent for a few minutes until I saw my dad stand up. Both mom and I looked up at him. He rubbed his chin then ran his hands through his hair. I could see that he was nervous, anxious, and broken hearted.

"I can't." He said; still not looking at us. "I can't do this. I can't... this is too much."

"What do you mean?" My mom asked him as she stood up and placed her hand on his arm.

"I can't just stand here and watch my daughter die. I can't do it." He looked at my mom straight into her eyes.

"Do not say that!" My mom practically yelled on the verge of tears. "My daughter will not die. She is a strong girl and will fight this! She will be treated and everything will be okay."

My dad laughed humorlessly. "We don't have the money to treat her, Celia." He said angrily.

"We'll think of something." She said in a low voice. It was like she was trying to convince herself more than anyone else.

Dad ran his hand through his hair then looked at me. He saw my tear streaked face and his features softened. "I'm sorry, please forgive me." He whispered then looked at my mom one last time before opening the door and walking out.

That fateful day, my dad did not just walk out the door, but out of our lives as well.

Chapter 1 - Private Lap Dance

My body moved on its own accord to the pulsing music. I closed my eyes and got lost in the music as I swayed my hips from side to side. I cupped each breast in one hand and moved my body up and down, slowly and seductively. I ran my hands down my body before cupping my breasts once more. I danced and gyrated until the end of the song then opened my eyes and looked at the rowdy crowd that were screaming and clapping their hands.

"More, more!" Everyone yelled as they threw dollars bills on the dance floor.

I took a bow and went behind the curtains. I took a deep breath of relief as soon as I was out of sight and started walking towards the dressing room.

"Trixie" I heard someone yell my name. I turned around and watched as Connor, the strip club manager, walked towards me. "You're needed for a private dance." He told me.

I shook my head. "No, no. You know that I don't do private dances."

"I'm not giving you a choice, Trixie. He is a wealthy customer."

"I'm not doing it. Can't you ask someone else?" I asked him; getting angry.

"No, you either do it or you're fired." He said; his tone firm and cold.

I wanted to scream out and tell him that I quit, but I knew I had no choice so instead, I asked. "Which room?"

Connor told me which room and walked away. I stood there for a second trying to gather myself. Connor knew that I didn't give private dances, but when it came to money, he apparently couldn't care less.

I straightened myself and took a deep breath before walking to the room. As I entered the room, my eyes met striking blue ones and I couldn't look away. I slowly walked towards him, making sure to sway my hips in a seductive manner. The music suddenly filled my ears and I started dancing exactly like I did a few moments ago. I forgot that he was there and lost myself to the music; it was as if my body had a mind of its own. The man then gestured with his finger for me to come closer. I gulped and walked even closer towards him. He suddenly placed his hands on my waist while I kept on swaying seductively. He brought me even closer to him and pulled me down onto his lap so that I was straddling him. He placed his hands on my butt; pulling me closer to him, and I started to grind against him. The man moaned and tilted his head back in enjoyment. I placed my hands on his chest as I grinded even more. He tilted his head back up and looked at me then his hands suddenly disappeared behind my back. Before I knew it, He had already undone the hooks of my bra and slid the straps down my arms before he tossed it away. I shook my breasts in his face before leaning all the way back as he held onto my waist with one hand while the other ran down the center of my chest. I came back up and leaned over then whispered in his ear.

"Would you like me to carry on?"

I could see the want and hunger in his eyes as he just nodded. I stood up then sat back down on his laps, but this time my back facing him. I grinded against him and I could feel him growing hard. I stood up and stood between his open legs and danced some more. Going up and down, swaying from side to side, and letting myself get lost in those blue eyes of his.

"Thank you." He said as soon as the third song ended.

I trailed my hand down his cheek then stood up. "Seventy five dollars" I told him as I outstretched my hand.

He grabbed his wallet from inside his pocket and placed five hundred dollars in my hand. I looked at the money then looked up at him; trying to figure out if he had lost his mind. He just looked at me with a smirk on his face. I bent down and grabbed my bra from the floor and started walking out of the room when I heard him call out.

"Wait a minute."

I turned around and looked at him. I watched as he stood up and walked towards me. The way he walked, the way he dressed; he oozed power.

"What's your name?" He whispered seductively.

"Trixie" I answered coolly even though my heart was beating fast. I then turned back around and walked out of the room before he could say anything else.

I walked to the dressing room where I found Connor waiting for me. I handed him the money then grabbed a towel that was hanging from my vanity mirror and dried myself.

"Not bad." Connor commented as he looked up at me.

I didn't reply and just grabbed my jeans and started dressing then grabbed my top and put it on as well.

"You know, I don't know why you insist on not doing private dances. You're really good. You're a money maker too." He told me grinning.

My face expression was stone cold as I grabbed my bag and outstretched my hand. "Just give me my share of the money so that I could go home."

He handed me four hundred dollars and took one hundred dollars for the house fees. I took my money with more force than necessary and walked out.

Joe, one of the bodyguards at the strip club, walked me out like he always did at the end of each night and hailed a taxi for me. He opened the taxi door and said.

"Have a good night, Trixie."

"Thank you, Joe." I gave him a small smile then got in the taxi.

#

I opened the door and closed it behind me as quietly as I could; careful not to wake up my mom and sister. I walked to the kitchen and grabbed a glass of water then walked to my room. I changed into my pajamas and was about to go to sleep when I heard a knock on my door. I walked to the door and opened it. Rosalinda stood there with a small smile on her face.

"Rosa, what are you doing up? It's late." I told her.

"I can't sleep." She told me with a shrug.

"Come, let's talk inside before mom wakes up." I whispered then stepped aside for her to come in.

She sat down on my bed and I took a seat beside her. She started playing with her fingers as if nervous.

"What's wrong, honey?" I asked her softly. "You can tell me."

"It's just..." She looked up at me as a tear slid down her cheeks. "Everyone's treating me differently at school. I'm known as the girl who has cancer."

I held my sister's hand and looked straight into her eyes. "Don't let them get to you, Rosa. You are a brave girl."

"A lot of people have stopped talking to me. I barely have any friends left."

"Then they were never your friends to begin with, honey. You know who your true friends are when you go through a tough phase like this."

"Do you think it's a phase?" She asked me hesitantly in a low voice.

"I don't think. I know." I assured her, even though I was trying to assure myself more than anyone. "I know that my sister is a tough girl and will get through anything!" I gave her a small reassuring smile and squeezed her hand.

Rosalinda leaned forward and crushed me in a hug. "I love you, Es." Her voice sounded muffled.

"I love you too, Rosa. Never forget that." I told her as I pulled back. "Now, go back to sleep, it's late."

She nodded and stood up from the bed then walked to the door. She looked back at me and gave me a small smile before walking out.

You forgot to take a shower. My mind told me. I stood up and walked to my bathroom then stripped off my pajamas and threw them in the laundry hamper. I then walked to the shower, turned on the water, and stood underneath the flowing water that ran down my back. I closed my eyes for a moment as I relished in the feeling of hot water on my body. I opened my eyes and grabbed my sponge then poured body wash on it and started scrubbing it all over my body; trying to remove all of the dirty looks and touches I got. I felt so dirty. I then poured a little bit of shampoo on my hand and washed my hair before stepping out of the shower. I dried myself off with a towel before wrapping it around my body and walking back out to my room. Opening my dresser, I grabbed my old and comfy pajamas and put it on then lay on my bed. It wasn't long before I was in deep sleep.

#

I tried to rub the sleep out of my eyes as I walked out of my room the next morning. I walked in to the kitchen and saw my mom cooking up breakfast in her work uniform.

"Good morning, mom."

"Morning" She told me. "Why are you up early? You should get some sleep." I shrugged and took a seat at the kitchen table. "I don't get why you have to work at night. Why can't you work an afternoon shift?" She asked me.

My mom hated the idea of me working night shifts. She thought that it was too dangerous.

"They need waitresses to work the night shift, mom." I lied.

My mom didn't know that I worked as a stripper and I wasn't going to tell her. We weren't overly religious people or anything, but it wasn't something I was proud to talk about nor was it something my mother would be happy to know. Saving her the heartache, I simply told her that I was working at a diner.

"I don't like you going out at night all alone."

"We already talked about this, mom." I told her. "Where is Rosa?" I asked her; changing the subject.

"She's in her room getting ready for school." I nodded and just then Rosalinda appeared in the kitchen; holding her back pack.

My mom placed three plates of pancakes in front of us then sat down and ate as well. After we finished eating, she placed the plates in the sink and was about to wash them when I stopped her.

"Go. I'll do it."

She nodded and grabbed her keys to her old blue beetle from the counter and turned to Rosalinda. "Are you ready, sweetie?" She asked her.

Rosalinda nodded and stood up from her seat. She fixed her backpack before walking towards me and kissing my cheek. "Bye, sis"

"Bye, have a good day." I said with a wide smile as I watched both my mom and sister walk out.

**********Remember to vote, comment, share, recommend, add 'Trixie' to your reading list, and follow. :)

Chapter 2 - Meeting the Client

"Connor wants you in his office now." Coco, one of the many strippers at the club, informed me and didn't even wait for me to reply as she just kept walking.

I had just gotten off the stage and was about to go to the dressing room to change, but instead I walked to Connor's office and knocked on the door.

"Come in."

I walked inside and saw Connor sitting behind his desk looking at some papers. He looked up at me with a grin on his face.

"You were asking for me?"

"Yes." He said as he stood up. "You're needed for a private dance again."

"What? No. I'm not doing it. You know I don't do private dances."

"Well, you did do one yesterday." He retorted.

"It was an exception." I all but yelled. "You practically forced me. You didn't give me a choice. Did you?"

"I don't care." He said in an overly cool tone as he walked towards me. "I have already gotten paid a thousand dollars." I looked up at him wide eyed. "Yes you heard right." He said smugly as he held out a wad of cash. "This is for you." He held out the cash for me to take. "Now go put on something nice. He's waiting for you in the VIP room."

Without replying, I grabbed the cash from his hand and walked out, making sure to forcefully slam the door behind me. I walked to the dressing room and grabbed a black deep cowl neck backless mini dress and put it on then made my way to the VIP room. One of the bodyguards gave me a smile and opened the door for me to enter. I stepped inside and froze in my spot as the same blue eyes from the night before looked at me.

He gestured with his finger for me to come closer. "Come here." His voice was full of power and authority and I couldn't help but walk over to him.

I stood in front of him and he made no movement nor did he say a word. He just stared at me with dark eyes, so I started moving my hips slowly from side to side then tugged at the end of my dress and started to pull it up when I heard his gruff voice halting my actions.

"Stop" I let my hands fall to my sides and looked at him questioningly. "Sit" He ordered and I did as told. "Closer" He ordered once more and I scooted closer. "What's your name?" He asked me.

"Trixie" I said, wanting my voice to come out strong, but instead it came out as a mere whisper. "I already told you that."

"Let me rephrase that." He said in low voice that sent shivers down my spine as he leaned forward. "What's your real name?"

"Trixie" I repeated meekly.

The man smirked and leaned back. "I don't appreciate people lying to me." He told me, but I didn't respond. "Stand up." Once again I did as told. I never listened to anyone, not even the customers, but for some reason the way he spoke made me want to comply with his orders. "Dance for me." He instructed. "But, keep the dress on."

I nodded and started swinging my hips from left to right in a figure eight then let my hands wander up and down my body as I made eye contact with those blue fierce eyes. Lifting both of my hands over my head, I sensually traced my left fingertips down my right arm, across my chest, and down the left side of my body then used my right arm to trace the right side of my body. I walked closer to him, sat down on his lap with my back to him, and tossed my head back letting my hair trickle down his chest then started grinding into him. I scooted back a little so that my butt was against his package and started grinding in circles. Slowly, I lowered myself from his lap and on to the floor; putting my hands on his legs for support. I got on my hands and knees, and crawled away from him then arched my back so my butt was sticking up in the air and looked over my shoulder and saw him leaning forward with wide eyes. I bit my lip and got off the floor by bracing both of my hands on the ground and sticking my butt up first then traced the back of my legs with my fingertips as I rolled up to stand. I strutted back over to him and straddled his lap; each leg on one side and placed my hands on his chest then bent my chest down so that my breasts were in his face before coming up slowly. I ran my hands through his hair and leaned over so that my mouth was beside his ear. I licked his earlobes then whispered, "Do you want me to go on?" Then leaned back and looked at him.

"No." He said; his voice strained and hoarse.

I started to stand up from his lap, but he placed his hand on my waist pulling me back down to him.

"I want you to stay like this." I hesitantly nodded. He looked straight into my eyes before saying. "Tell me about yourself."

I smiled seductively. "Why don't you tell me something about yourself first?" I asked him; trying to stall. I didn't talk about myself or my private life to the customers. It was simply off limits.

"Okay, what would you like to know?" He asked me.

"Let's start with your name."

"You don't know who I am?" He asked me in a surprised tone.

"Should I know who you are?"

He shook his head. "Collin Edwards."

"What do you do, Collin?" I asked him.

"I'm the owner and CEO of Edwards Inc." He said proudly. "Now, tell me about you."

"First, I'd like to know one thing." I said as I stared straight into his eyes.

"What do you want to know?"

"Why didn't you want me to take off my dress as I danced for you?" It was a very reasonable question considering all of the men that came here wanted to see skin, yet Collin didn't.

"I'm not interested in your body as much as I'm interested in you." He trailed his finger on my bottom lip and I involuntarily parted my mouth.

Just then the bodyguard opened the door and poked his head inside to check on us before his head disappeared and he closed the door.

"I think our time's up." I told him with a grin as I started to stand up. This time he let me. I started walking out when his voice stopped me.

"I want to see you." He said.

I turned around. "That is what you're doing, no?" I asked him as I looked up at him with a raised eyebrow.

"I meant outside of your job."

"Sorry, Collin" I looked up at him. "I don't go out with customers nor do I have the time." I told him then turned back around and started to walk out the door before he could even say anything.

I walked to the dressing room and changed my clothes before heading out of the strip club. Joe hailed a taxi for me and I got in. I looked out the window and thought about Collin. It wasn't the first time one of the customers had asked me out and I had said no, but I didn't know why I got the feeling that Collin was different. He didn't even want me to take my dress off. Sure the night before I did take my dress off for him, but I couldn't help but feel that there was something different about him; a good kind of different. I shrugged off the thought. I would never go out with him or any other customer for that matter and like I told him I didn't have the time. I had my sister to worry about.

The taxi stopped in front of my house. I paid him and stepped out of the car. Getting my keys out of my bag, I opened the door as quietly as I could, walked inside the house then closed the door behind me. I slipped off my heels and held them in my hand then walked in to my bedroom and quietly closed the door then walked in to my bathroom, stripped off my clothes, and hopped in the shower. I closed my eyes and tilted my head up; letting the water fall over my face before flowing all over my body.

I turned the water off and stepped out of the shower and wrapped myself in a towel and walked back in to my bedroom. I opened my dresser and pulled out my old flannel pyjama and put it on then lay down on the bed and willed the thoughts to go away before falling asleep.

#

"There's no milk." I said to no one in particular and groaned.

I had woken up the next day, to an empty house, feeling famished. I decided on eating cereal, but there was no milk in the fridge. Mom had probably forgotten to buy.

I opened the cupboard and noticed that we needed to stock up on a lot of things. I groaned once more and walked back to my room. I opened my closet and grabbed random jeans and top and put them on then slipped on my old sneakers and tied the shoelaces before going over to my nightstand and picking up a scrunchie, tying back my hair in a ponytail. I shoved some money into my pockets then walked out of the house.

The grocery store was right around the corner so I thought I'd just walk and breathe in some fresh air; god knew I needed it.

I entered the store and grabbed a basket then went to the produce aisle first.

A little while later, I had brought just about everything except what I came here for; milk. I started walking over to the dairy aisle when I stopped in front of the chocolates aisle. I decided to bring home some chocolate; maybe a Cadbury. Rosalinda hadn't been eating properly lately since she had lost her appetite so maybe a Cadbury could do the trick. I knew just how much she loved her Cadburys. I placed several chocolate bars in the basket then walked over to the dairy aisle.

"At last" I said in a relieved tone as I picked up a bottle of milk and looked at it like it was some prized possession. I heard someone chuckling behind me and turned around. I almost dropped the milk to the floor as I saw who was there. "Collin?"

**********Remember to vote, comment, share, recommend, add 'Trixie' to your reading list, and follow. :)

Chapter 3 - Unexpected Breakfast

"Collin?" My tone was surprised.

Collin looked at me with a smirk on his face. "Hello, Trixie."

"What are you doing here?" I asked him stupidly.

His smirk grew even wider as he said. "The same thing you're doing; buying groceries."

My gaze went to the basket full of grocery items that he held in his hand.

"I didn't know you lived in this neighborhood." I said; scrunching my eyebrows together trying to remember if I had seen him in the neighborhood before.

"I don't." He answered in a clipped tone, not giving me any more information.

It was awkwardly silent for a brief second before I said. "I have to get going." I gave him a small smile and started to walk away when his voice stopped me.

"Wait a second." I turned around and looked at him with a raised eyebrow. "Do you want to grab a cup of coffee?" He asked me hopefully.

I shook my head. "I already told you that I don't go out with customers."

"I'm not asking you out." He argued. "Just two friends having a cup of coffee, is that so wrong?" He asked me.

"No." I shook my head. "Except we're not friends" I gave him a smile and started to walk away when once again he stopped me.

"Then we could be friends." He retorted.

I turned around and looked at him. Determination was clear in his eyes. I knew that he wasn't going to take no for an answer.

"Fine" I agreed. "But, you're buying me breakfast." Collin gave me a wide smile and nodded.

"Is that all?" The cashier, a young woman in her mid twenties, at the grocery store asked me and I nodded. "That will be fifty dollars." She informed me as she looked up at me with a kind smile.

I shoved my hand inside my pocket to bring out the money when Collin suddenly outstretched his arm and handed the young woman his Black Visa Card.

"No, no." I pulled the change from my pocket, but before I could hand it to the young woman, Collin grabbed my hand; stopping me.

"Don't argue." He instructed; his tone gave out authority and made me not want to argue with him so I just nodded and placed the money back inside my pocket.

Collin held my plastic bags along with his own as well as we walked to his car. He handed the bags to who I assumed was his driver and we waited for him as he placed them in the trunk of the car then came back to our side and opened the door. I stood there for a moment not making a move to get inside the car. I was wary about him taking me anywhere since I didn't know him that well; if at all.

"Aren't you going to get in?" Collin asked me with a raised eyebrow.

I was quiet for a moment as I tried to figure out what to tell him. "Um... there's a coffee shop down the street." I murmured.

Collin studied me for a moment before speaking. "Okay." He turned to his driver and spoke with him in a hushed tone before he turned back to me.

"Let's go."

"I should grab my groceries." I said as I gestured to the trunk of his car.

"No, leave them." He ordered. "We'll come back for them before I take you back home." I hesitantly nodded and we started walking towards the coffee shop.

We entered the coffee shop and I noticed that it was empty except for one table. We found a table beside the window and sat down. The waitress approached us with a smile on her face and took our orders. Once she left, Collin leaned back in his chair and stared at me as if trying to figure something out.

"You don't trust me." He stated.

"I don't know you." I retorted.

Just then the waitress arrived with our orders. She placed the latte and croissant I had ordered in front of me on the table then placed the coffee that Collin had ordered in front of him as well.

"Enjoy." She said with a smile before walking away.

I took a sip of my latte and moaned in approval. I noticed Collin looking at me with an amused smile, and I suddenly felt my cheeks heat up. I smiled shyly then placed the latte back on the table. I held the croissant and tore off a bite size then placed it in my mouth. It tasted so good that it sent my eyes rolling to the back of my head.

"That good?" I heard Collin ask.

I nodded embarrassingly. "Would you like to try it?" I asked him and he shook his head.

"No, I already had my breakfast." He said and I nodded. "I want to know more about you." He said; his eyes never leaving mine.

I grabbed a tissue paper from the table and wiped my mouth with it before replying. "There's nothing to know."

"Entertain me, though." He said. "What does your mother do?"

Why does he want to know that? I thought to myself, but answered nonetheless. "She works as a maid at an inn just down the road."

Collin nodded then asked. "What about your father?"

I felt like someone had poured cold water all over me, and my whole body stiffened. "Why do you want to know all of those stuff?" I asked him sounding irritated.

"I just want to get to know you a little bit better." He answered, sounding genuine.

"My dad left us about a year ago." I said as I looked straight into his eyes; waiting for him to say something.

Collin, however, didn't comment on the subject instead he just nodded and took a sip of his coffee. He probably noticed my change in demeanour so he decided not to inquire into the matter anymore, and for that I was grateful.

It was silent after that and I took the chance to finish my croissant peacefully.

"Would you like another one?" Collin asked me as I pushed my empty plate away from me.

I shook my head. "No, thank you." I gave him a small smile then held the cup of latte in my hand and took a sip. It had gotten cold, but still tasted good nonetheless.

His phone suddenly rang. He checked who the caller was, but didn't answer the call. Instead he asked. "Are you ready to go?" I simply nodded.

Collin ordered the bill and paid then we both stood up. We exited the coffee shop and started walking towards his car. His driver probably noticed us walking back to the car because he stepped out of the car, came to the passenger's side and opened the door.

"I'll just walk back home." I told Collin.

"No. I'm driving you back home." He responded.

"It's not a problem, really. It's only a couple of blocks away." I argued.

Collin didn't need to say anything because the way he looked at me spoke louder than words ever could. His look told me not to argue with him and just get inside the car.

"It's the second home to the right." I pointed to the house. Collin's driver nodded and a moment later the car came to a halt in front of my house.

Collin opened the car door and stepped out. I was about to open mine when it suddenly flew open and my eyes met Collin's blue ones. I gave him a small smile and stepped out of the car. The driver had already unloaded the groceries from the trunk, but didn't hand them to me.

"I'll take it from here." I told him politely. He nodded and handed me the plastic bags. "Thank you." I gave him a small smile. He nodded once more then walked back to the front of the car; leaving Collin and I alone.

"Thank you for breakfast." I said as I shifted the grocery bags in my hand.

"My pleasure" He said with a wide smile.

I gave him a smile of my own and started to walk towards my house. I didn't turn around, but I could feel Collin's eyes on me as I opened the front door and stepped inside the house.

#

I was in the kitchen cooking up lunch when I heard the door open and a moment later mom and Rosalinda appeared in the kitchen.

"Hey, you two" I gave them a wide smile.

Rosalinda ran towards me and crushed me in a hug. I wrapped my arms around my sister and hugged her tight. I looked over at my mom who had a smile on her face.

"Come on, go and wash up before lunch." I told her once I pulled back. "I also have a surprise for you." I said in a sing song voice.

"What is it?" She asked me with a wide grin on her face.

"Wash up first." I told her and she nodded then walked to the bathroom.

"What did you get her?" My mom asked me as she walked closer towards me and peeked inside the pot that I was stirring.

"Her favorite chocolate; Cadbury."

My mom didn't have time to reply as Rosalinda reentered the kitchen and sat down at the kitchen table.

"So what did you get me?" She asked with a grin.

I placed a plate of chicken curry in front of her, and she looked up at me, the grin wiped off her face.

"I'm not hungry." She complained.

"You have to eat something, Rosa." She wanted to complain again, but I stopped her before she could. "Just a bit at least and then I'll tell you what I bought for you." I told her with a teasing smile.

She nodded and started eating. I placed two more plates on the table; one for me and one for my mom. We sat down and ate quietly. A little while later, Rosalinda pushed her plate away. I looked at her half full plate then looked at my mom who just nodded. At least she ate more than the day before. I stood up from my seat and opened the kitchen cupboard, brought out the Cadbury bar and hid it behind my back.

"Which hand?" I asked her with a cheeky smile.

"Just give it to me." She said exasperated.

I chuckled and handed her the chocolate bar. Just as I had expected, she ripped it open and started eating. I looked at my mom who was watching the scene in front of her with a smile on her face.

"Thank you, Es." Rosa hugged me.

"You're welcome, honey." I hugged my sweet little sister back.

**********Remember to vote, comment, share, recommend, add 'Trixie' to your reading list, and follow. :)

Chapter 4 - Private Dance for the Public Eye

"You're up next." Conner said as he peeked through the gap in the curtains out into the stage.

Just then the song ended and another one started; that was my cue for me to get on stage. Even though I had been doing it for quite some time, I still got nervous whenever it was my turn to get on stage. I took a deep breath then walked past the curtains. The crowd started cheering and clapping their hands giving me the courage to start moving my body, swaying my hips from side to side in a circular motion, running my hands up and down my body seductively. I played with the strings of my dress, and the crowd went wild.

"Lose the dress." One drunkard screamed.

I started teasing them, running my hands through the strings of my dress, but not removing them. One time, two times, eventually I slipped the left string down my arm followed by the right one, then the dress slipped easily down to my waist and pooled around my feet.

I bent down seductively and picked it up then turned around so that my back was facing the crowd and threw the dress over my shoulder just like a bride throws the bouquet over her shoulder on her wedding day for someone lucky to catch.

The crowd started cheering and I turned around to see who had caught my dress, and my eyes met blue familiar ones for a brief second before I looked down at his hands and saw him holding the dress with a smirk on his face. I hadn't seen him in about a week. I felt butterflies in my stomach for some reason.

I walked over to him slowly and seductively, making sure to sway my hips. I stood about two feet away from Collin with my feet hip width apart. I arched my back and started to draw circles with my hips. I slowly bent my knees and grinded down then up again, dancing erotically. I slowly turned around and gazed at Collin who was looking at me with wide eyes. My back still to him, I opened my legs gradually then bent over so that my bottom was brazenly in Collin's face. I bent one knee to the side then straightened the other one out to the side. I glided my hand up my straight leg and raised my head over my shoulder to take a look at Collin once again, and in a swift move; I slapped my bottom making the crowd go wild. I smirked and stood up seductively then walked backwards so that I was standing between his legs; my back still to him. I moved my body gracefully from side to side then placed my hands on his knees to support myself as I lowered my bottom towards his lap and grinded down gently; moving my hips in circular motions. I looked at Collin over my shoulder and smiled seductively then stood and turned around so that I was facing him. I caught one of his knees between my knees and gently rubbed up and down his thighs as I leaned forward and blew gently into his ear. I could hear him breathing heavily and I knew that he was turned on, and so was I. I stood up from my position and positioned myself between his knees then leaned forward and placed my hands on either side of his shoulders then put my legs on each of his thighs, lifted my torso, slid my knees into the space in front of his package and slid slowly all the way down so that I was kneeling on the floor. I placed my hands back on Collin's knees for support as I stood up sensually with my bottom up first and I arched my back so that my chest was in Collin's face. I turned around and walked back to the stage sexily, slowly, and seductively.

The crowd had gone wild. "More, more, more" they screamed.

I didn't notice anyone though, only Collin. My eyes went to him and I noticed how he was leaning forward looking at me; desire clear in his eyes. My lips turned upwards in a smile before I walked off the stage as two other strippers came on.

What did I just do? I thought to myself as soon as I was off the stage.

"Quite the show you put on out there." Conner said as I walked in to the dressing room with him on my heels.

"Bug off, Conner." I told him; not even looking at him as I grabbed my towel and dried myself off.

"Not a nice way to talk to your manager." He said in a sing song voice.

I turned around and looked at him through narrowed eyes. "What do you want, Conner?" I asked him, sounding irritated.

"A smile would be a start." He told me as he grinned. I looked at him with a raised eyebrow and his grin quickly disappeared. He cleared his throat then said "Here, this is for you." He handed me a wad of cash. "The tips for tonight."

I nodded and accepted the money then he walked out of the dressing room.

I changed into jeans and top, and held my bag in my hands then walked out of the dressing room, and as usual, Joe walked me out and hailed a taxi for me. I was about to step inside the taxi when I heard someone calling my name.

"Trixie"

I turned around and watched as Collin walked towards me with long, purposeful strides. Joe immediately stood in front of me in a protective manner.

"Who are you?" He quickly took his bodyguard stance.

"It's okay, Joe. He is a friend." Joe nodded and stood beside me.

Collin glared at Joe for a moment before he turned his gaze towards me.

"I'm taking you home." He didn't ask, he ordered.

"No, I'm taking a taxi home." I retorted.

"Don't argue with me, Trixie." He said in a voice full of authority then went to grab my hand when Joe once again instantly stood in front of me; effectively blocking Collin from me.

"She said she didn't want to go." Joe growled. He was in full bodyguard mode at that moment.

"Joe, it is fine. I'll go with him." I said trying to ease the tension of the situation since both men looked like they were ready to start a fight at any moment.

Joe looked at me over his shoulder. "Are you sure?" He asked me and I just nodded.

He silently stood beside me once more and Collin glared at him again before taking my hand, a bit forcefully, and walking me to his car. I saw his driver standing by the car. He greeted me once we approached him then opened the passenger's door.

"You surprised me." Collin said as his driver drove me back home. My cheeks flushed and I just gave him a small shy smile. "It was a good surprise though." He added.

"Are you always at strip clubs?" I asked him amused.

He chuckled. "No, I actually came to see you."

"Oh, what for?" I asked him.

"I missed you." He said as his hand slipped into mine, and I let him thread our fingers together. I looked at our intertwined hands and back up at him. It felt good; it felt like the perfect fit.

"Go out with me." He said.

"You never give up, do you?" I asked him with a teasing smile.

"Not when I want something, no." He answered sincerely.

"I already told you, Collin. I don't go out with customers."

I looked straight into his eyes. I could feel him getting slightly mad as he tightened his hold on my hand, but didn't say anything.

Suddenly the car came to a halt, and Collin released his hand from mine.

"I'm picking you up for dinner tomorrow night."

"I already told you...." I started, but Collin interrupted me.

"It's final." He said in a tone of finality.

"I have work." I argued one last time.

"I'll pick you up at seven, we'll have dinner and then I'll drop you off at work." He said as he stared at me; daring me to oppose him.

I knew I wasn't going to win this argument. "Fine" I agreed then opened the car door and stepped out.

I walked to the front door, opened my purse and brought out the house keys. I was about to open the door when I felt someone place his hand on my arm. I jumped back, frightened, and turned around only to be met with a smirking Collin.

"You forgot this." He said as he handed me the dress that he had caught earlier at the strip club.

I looked at the dress for a moment then back up at Collin. He was staring at me intently.

"Keep it." I told him in a seductive voice then walked inside the house, closing the door behind a stunned Collin.

I walked to my bedroom and sat down on my bed for a moment as I thought about what had just happened. I had agreed to go out on a date with Collin. I had never agreed to going out with any of the customers before. Why did I agree to the date with Collin? He felt different. He wasn't like the rest. I could feel it. I hoped I wasn't wrong about him though. I sighed, stood up from the bed and walked to the bathroom. I stripped off my clothes and took a hot shower.

I lay down on my bed after the long, hot, and relaxing bath. I looked up at the ceiling unable to sleep as I thought about my date with Collin. It didn't matter anyways because I knew that our relationship would go nowhere.

**********Remember to vote, comment, share, recommend, add 'Trixie' to your reading list, and follow. :)

Chapter 5 - Dinner and the Beach

I sat in front of my vanity mirror as I put the finishing touches of my makeup. I was getting ready for my date with Collin, and for some reason I was actually excited about it. Suddenly, I heard a knock on my door.

"Come in."

I watched, from my vanity mirror, as Rosalinda opened the door and walked inside my room then sat down on my bed. I turned around in my chair and gave my sister a small smile.

"Is everything okay?" I asked her.

"Yeah" She said dejectedly. "Mom is watching some documentary on TV, and I'm bored."

"Do you want me to take you out somewhere before I go to work?" I asked her. I would gladly cancel my date for my sister.

"No, you have a date." She told me.

I stood up, walked to her, and sat down beside her on the bed. "I don't care about the date, Rosa. You're more important."

She shook her head. "No, it is fine. I'll go to bed in a little while anyways." I nodded then stood up and sat back in front of my vanity mirror. "You look pretty." She commented then added. "I wish I could be pretty like you."

I turned around in my chair and looked at my sister; she had a sad look on her face. I stood up, walked back to her, and hugged her sideways.

"You are the prettiest girl I have ever met, Rosa. Don't you ever forget that, okay?" She looked down at her laps; the sad look still plastered on her face. "I need makeup to look pretty." I told her. "You're naturally beautiful, sweetie."

She looked up at me through her lashes and wrapped her arms around my neck; hugging me tightly.Suddenly we heard the doorbell ring. Rosalinda pulled back and looked at me.

"Your date's here." She said with a grin.

I stood in front of my floor length mirror and smoothed my navy dress.

"Just go see him. You look nice." She said exasperated.

I laughed and turned to her. "Don't you want to come and meet him?" I asked her.

She shook her head no. I knew she was not okay with meeting new people ever since she was diagnosed with cancer, so I didn't pressure her. I walked over to her and pulled her into a brief hug.

"If you need anything call me, okay?" I told her once I pulled back and she nodded with a wide smile.

"Have fun." I heard her say as I walked out of the room.

I found my mom and Collin talking at the front door. Collin looked up at me and his lips slowly turned upwards into a small smile.

"Hey." I greeted him and he blinked twice as if coming out of a stupor.

"Hey, are you ready?" He asked me with a wide smile and I nodded.

I turned to my mom. "I'm going to work afterwards so don't wait up." She nodded. I kissed her cheek then walked out with Collin.

Collin walked me to his car and opened the passenger-side door for me to get in then went to the other side and got in the driver's seat.

"Where is your driver?" I asked him as he drove us to our destination for the night.

"I told him to go home." He answered; not looking at me, but at the road ahead.

"Why?" I asked him as I turned my body sideways to look at him.

"I wanted us to be alone tonight; just you and me." He said as he looked sideways at me with a heartwarming smile on his face.

I gave him a smile of my own then looked out the window. Suddenly, I felt his hand on mine. I looked up at him and saw him not looking at me, but still looking at the road ahead. He probably noticed my gaze on him because he looked sideways at me then raised my hand and placed a sweet kiss there. I looked out the window as my cheeks flushed.

It was funny how I was a stripper that danced practically naked for men's enjoyment, yet Collin could make my cheeks flush with just a simple gesture.

The car finally came to a stop in front of a fancy looking restaurant. One of the valet parking men opened the door for me and I stepped out of the car. I saw Collin handing another one of the men his car keys then he came around to my side and placed his arm tightly around my waist before we walked inside the restaurant.

"Good evening, Mr. Edwards." The hostess greeted Collin. "Your table's this way." She said formally as she started leading us towards the table.

"This is... nice." I commented as I looked around the restaurant and noticed how everyone looked like they came from money.

"You're not comfortable." Collin stated.

I looked at him. "No, no. I am." I lied through my teeth.

"I think we already established the fact that I don't appreciate people lying to me." He said as he leaned forward and clasped his hands together on the table.

Luckily, I was saved by the waiter who handed us the menus. I looked at the menu and my eyes widened at the prices. Each plate cost almost as much as I made every night at the strip club.

"Do you know what you want to order?" Collin asked me.

I looked up at him. "Um... why don't you just order for the both of us?"

Collin smirked and nodded then gestured for the waiter to come. He gave him our orders then the waiter left. Collin leaned back in his chair and stared at me intently.

"Why are you looking at me like that?" I asked him, suddenly feeling self conscious.

"You look very beautiful." He complimented.

"Thank you." I smiled shyly.

"So tell me, Trixie." He leaned forward and placed his arms on the table. "Why do work as a stripper?"

"For the money" I answered honestly; I wasn't going to lie.

"Why don't you work something else? Why stripping?" He asked and before I could answer he added. "Is it because it's easy money?"

I scoffed. "Easy?" I asked in disbelief. "It is anything but easy. I have to deal with groping, hand roaming, and a lot of rejection. I have to live a certain lifestyle so that I don't gain weight. There's also the stress of not knowing how much you're going to make."

Just then the waiter arrived with our food; stopping me from my ranting. He placed the plates in front of me and Collin.

"Enjoy." He said then walked away.

I watched as Collin cut into the juicy steak he had ordered and placed it in his mouth. I started cutting into mine as well when I heard him ask.

"Then why do you do it?"

I stopped cutting and looked up at him. "I already told you..."

"For the money" He interrupted me. "That's not what I mean." He said.

"Then what do you mean?" I asked him as I looked at him questioningly.

"Is the money that well for you to keep working in a job that you apparently hate?" He asked as he took another bite of the steak.

"Honestly, yes" I said as I placed a bite of the steak in my mouth as well. It helped me pay for Rosalinda's treatment expenses, and my sister's wellbeing was way more important than my happiness. I added quietly in my head, but I wasn't going to tell him that though.

Collin nodded, but didn't comment even though I could feel that he wanted to say something.

"So when do you usually get some down time?" He asked me a few minutes later.

"On Saturdays and Sundays since I only work five days a week"

Collin nodded again and we ate the rest of our food in silence. Once we were done the waiter came and picked up our empty plates and asked if we wanted desserts, but I kindly declined.

"Are you sure? They make the best desserts here." Collin said; trying to convince me.

I shook my head. "No, thanks" I declined once more.

Collin looked at his watch and asked me what time I had to be at work and I told him at ten. He gestured for the waiter to get the bill. After he had paid, we walked out of the restaurant.

"Where are we going now?" I asked him once I noticed that we were driving down an unfamiliar road to me.

"Since we still have a little bit of time before I have to take you to work, I thought we could go to the beach." He said and I nodded.

A little while later, the car came to a halt at a parking space near the beach. Collin stepped out of the car and quickly came around to my side and opened my door. He held my hand in his as we walked down the beach. The smell of the ocean, the sound of the waves, it was so relaxing; it was literally a breath of fresh air.

Collin suddenly stopped walking and sat down on the sand; not caring that his most probably expensive suit would get dirty. He pulled me down to him, I gasped at the sudden move, and he sat me down on his lap then wrapped his arms around me. He placed his head at the top of my shoulder as we both stared at the mesmerising ocean.

"I'm taking you out on Saturday." He said. "I want to spend the day with you."

I turned my head sideways and looked at him with an amused smile on my face. "I think you have a problem with asking." I told him and he just shrugged.

I didn't mind the thought of spending Saturday with him though so I didn't argue. I turned back around and once again lost myself to the beautiful sight of the waves crashing against the shore.

About a moment later, he said "I don't want to take you to work." I turned sideways and looked at him with a raised eyebrow. "I hate the idea of drunken men ogling your body."

I didn't reply because I had to admit that I hated the way those drunken men ogled my body too, but I had to do it for my sister. Suddenly, in a surprise move, I turned around in Collin's lap and stared into his blue eyes. I could just get lost in those beautiful blue eyes of his.

Collin slowly leaned forward and pressed his lips against mine. I parted my lips ever so slightly, giving him more access. He wasted no time as he slipped his tongue inside my mouth and swirled it around. He tasted so good. He placed his hands on my ass and pulled me closer to him. A mixture of sensations passed through my body. Pulling back, I looked at him; desire swirling in his eyes.

"I need to go to work." I told him breathlessly and he begrudgingly nodded.

He pulled me off his lap and I stood up. He then stood up as well and held my hand as we walked back to his car.

**********Remember to vote, comment, share, recommend, add 'Trixie' to your reading list, and follow. :)

Chapter 6 - Ice Skating and Wannabe

My room was a mess!

My closet door was open and clothes were scattered all over my bed.

I was spending the day with Collin, and I had no idea what to wear. He just said that we would be spending Saturday together, but he gave me no clue whatsoever to where we would be going.

I walked over to my nightstand and picked up my phone and started writing a text message to Collin.

He had asked for my phone number on our first date and I thought there was no harm in giving it to him.

'Where are we going?' I wrote then pressed the send button.

A few minutes later, my phone pinged.

'Places.' The text message read.

I shook my head in amusement at his reply before writing 'I need to know what to wear.'

'Something comfortable, and bring a jacket with you.'

I placed my phone back on the nightstand and looked at the clothes that were sprawled all over my bed. Just then, my door creaked open, and Rosalinda slipped in.

"Where are you going?" She asked me curiously.

"I'm spending the day with Collin." I told her with a smile.

"Oh." She said disappointed.

"Is something wrong?" I asked her.

She shook her head and sat on my vanity mirror chair. "I wanted to ask you if you could take me out to watch a movie or something."

"Of course I'll take you out."

"You just said that you're going out with Collin." She stated with a confused look on her face.

"Who cares about him?" I waved my hand. "We could watch a movie then get ice cream later on, chocolate and peanut butter your favorite." I said excitedly.

"No, we'll go some other time. It's fine." She said with a small smile then stood up from her seat.

"No, we are going out." I insisted. "We haven't gone out in a long time."

Rosalinda's smile widened, but then suddenly she frowned. "What about Collin?"

"I can go out with him some other time."

"He... he can come along if you want." She said hesitantly.

I looked at my sister for a moment trying to see if she meant what she had said. I knew that she had been self conscious ever since she was diagnosed with Leukemia. Her hair loss was what had gotten her down the most.

"He doesn't have to come." I assured her.

"No, I want him to come. I don't mind." She assured me before adding "at least that way I won't feel very guilty that I ruined your plans."

I chuckled then walked over to my sister and placed my hands on her arms. "Okay, but if you feel the bit least uncomfortable then we leave, okay?" She nodded with a small smile. "Now, help me choose something to wear." I grinned at her.

Half an hour later, I was dressed up in a knit tunic and black leggings while Rosalinda went back to her room to change.

I was sitting at my vanity mirror applying my makeup when Rosalinda opened the door, walked in, and sat on my bed as she watched me apply my makeup.

"Can I put on some makeup as well?" She asked me.

I turned in my chair and looked at my sister who was smiling hopefully at me. "You're a young and beautiful girl, why do you need makeup?" I asked her and she just shrugged. I couldn't say no to her. "Come and sit here." I said as I stood up from my seat.

Rosalinda jumped off the bed; the smile still plastered on her face and sat down at the chair I had just vacated. I didn't go overboard with her and just applied a little bit of blush, mascara, and lip gloss.

"Done" I announced with a smile.

Rosalinda looked at herself in the mirror and her lips turned upwards in a smile. "I look nice." She admitted.

"You look more than nice."

She wrapped her arms around me and hugged me tight. "Thank you." Her voice sounded muffled through my hair.

The doorbell then rang and we pulled back from the hug.

"He's here." I said as I grabbed my ivory colored coat from the bed and walked out of the room with Rosalinda behind me.

Mom had already opened the door and was laughing at something Collin had said. He must have heard our footsteps because he looked up at us and a smile made its way to his face.

"Hi." I greeted him with a smile of my own.

"Hey." He walked towards me and placed a kiss on my cheek making color rise to my cheeks.

His gaze went to my sister and I totally forgot that she was there. "Sorry, I forgot to introduce you. This is my sister, Rosalinda."

Collin looked over at my sister who was standing behind me. "Hey, Rosalinda"

"Hey." She replied shyly.

"Rosalinda is coming with us if that's okay." I informed him.

Luckily, he didn't show any signs of disapproval. Instead, he gave us a wide smile.

"Of course, come on then let's go. We've got a great day ahead."

"Did you have breakfast?" Collin asked us as soon as we got inside his car. I shook my head no and I looked back at Rosalinda who mocked my action.

"First stop, breakfast" He said with a grin.

About half an hour later, the car came to a stop in front of a snazzy looking diner. We stepped outside the car, walked inside the diner, and sat at one of the empty tables. The waitress handed us three menus before walking away.

"What would you like to order?" Collin asked us as he looked up from the menu.

"Belgian waffles with bananas, strawberries, blueberries, and whipped cream." Rosalinda said with a shy smile. I smiled at my sister.

"What about you, Trixie?" Collin asked me.

"Trixie?" Rosalinda asked me with a questioning look on her face.

I looked at Collin with wide eyes and said. "Yeah, it's an inside joke between us. Right, Collin?" I pleaded with my eyes for him to go along with my lie.

"Yeah, yeah right" He smiled nervously.

"I'll have the same as my sister just without the whipped cream." I said quickly changing the subject.

Collin nodded then gestured for the waitress to come. He gave her our orders and ordered a plate of pancakes and bacon for him. It was awkwardly silent for a moment before I broke the silence.

"Where are we going after this?"

Collin smirked. "You'll see."

The food came a little while later and we ate and talked a bit. As soon as we finished, Collin paid the bill and we walked out of the diner. I handled the radio as Collin drove us to our destination. I started changing the stations until I settled on a channel that played only old tunes, and the tune that they were playing at that moment was just perfect; wannabe by the spice girls.

I looked back at my sister and we both smirked before we started belting out the song. At that moment, I forgot about Collin and just had fun. Once the song finished I looked at my sister who had started to relax a bit and then at Collin who was looking sideways at me with a sweet smile on his face. He didn't say anything though; he just intertwined his hand with mine and kept driving.

"No way!" Rosalinda said in a low, excited voice so that I would only hear.

"Do you like the place?" Collin asked us. I looked up at him like he was crazy.

I loved it.

Collin had brought us to an ice skating rink. I had never been at an ice skating rink before where as Rosalinda had been to one several times.

Collin rented three pairs of skates. I helped lace up Rosalinda's boots as Collin helped lace up mine. Rosalinda had no problem at all as she stood up and stepped onto the ice. Collin helped me stand up and we as well stepped onto the ice. He held both of my hands and helped me skate around. I had an advantage at my side since I was a stripper and I was flexible, but I wasn't going to tell Collin that. I liked the way his hands felt on mine, the way he led me around the ring. I looked at Rosalinda who was drifting along the ice rink like a butterfly; she was wonderful. She had a smile on her face. I hadn't seen her smile like that in a very long time. She saw me looking at her and she smiled then skated towards me and started skating around me.

Suddenly, my feet splayed, and I fell down on my bottom. Collin and Rosalinda started laughing while I just frowned at them. Collin cleared up his throat and started hoisting me up into a standing position. My feet splayed again and I clung onto him for dear life. I could see Collin trying to stifle a laugh while I just wanted to cry from hurt.

"Don't let go." I pleaded with Collin.

Rosalinda had disappeared from beside us and was skating around the ring.

"I would never let you go." He whispered softly as he looked straight into my eyes.

We started skating slowly around the ring while I stayed glued to Collin. I held his hand tightly; afraid that he would let go. My head was starting to hurt from concentrating so hard, and my jaw ached from gritting my teeth.

"Are you cold?" Collin asked me and I nodded.

We skated outside of the ring then sat down at a small bench. Collin wrapped his arm around me and pulled me closer to him. I clung onto him as I tried to get some warmth from him. I looked at the rink and noticed my sister skating around happily; not caring about the world.

"This was a fail." I heard Collin mutter.

I looked up at him through my lashes. "No, this was wonderful. Seeing my sister smile like this is wonderful. Thank you."

He seemed pleased with my answer as he gave me a wide smile and kissed my forehead. "Are you going to tell me?" He asked me.

"Tell you what?" I asked him confused.

"Your real name" He said. "It's obviously not Trixie, and don't you for a second think that I believed that it was your real name, but I thought that I would go along."

I gave him a guilty smile. I guess I could trust him. He did know where I lived. He knew my mother and my sister so a name wasn't going to hurt. "Esmeralda."

"Esmeralda." Collin tested the name out. "I like it, just like I like you."

I could feel my cheeks heating up and I grabbed a handful of his shirt and hid my face.

"Rosalinda doesn't know about your job as a stripper, right?" He asked me.

I looked back up at him. "No she doesn't."

"What about your mother?" He asked me.

"She doesn't know as well." He just looked at me, but didn't say anything. "Collin, please I don't want you to call me by my real name at the strip club."

There was a reason that I was using a stage name because if someone knew my real name it would put me in danger of being stalked and whatnot.

"I know, baby, I won't." The endearment didn't go unnoticed, but I decided not to comment on it. I just held a fistful of his shirt and scooted closer to him.

Rosalinda came tottering over to where we were sitting a little while later.

"That was awesome!" She exclaimed happily.

I couldn't help but smile at my sister's excitement. I was really happy that she was having fun.

"Do you want to stay for a little while longer?" Collin asked her and she shook her head no. "Then, come on. The day's still young. Let's do something else." He said as he stood up; taking up all the warmth with him.

**********Remember to vote, comment, share, recommend, add 'Trixie' to your reading list, and follow. :)

Chapter 7 - Hot Chocolates and Relationships

"Okay, I have nothing planned after this so you get to choose where you want to go next." Collin said as soon as we got inside his car.

I looked back at my sister who just shrugged then looked back at Collin. "Rosalinda was telling me earlier that she wanted to go to the movies." I told him, remembering that she had asked me that when we were at home. "If it is okay with you, that is" I added.

"Of course it's okay with me." He said with a wide smile. "Do you want to have lunch first?" He asked us and both of us shook our heads.

"I'm still feeling full from breakfast." I said.

"Me too" Rosalinda agreed.

About half an hour later, we arrived at the movie theater. Collin bought us tickets for a chick flick movie that Rosalinda and I wanted to watch. He wasn't very impressed about it, but it was very amusing seeing him sulk and pout, which was very weird considering he was serious all the time. We then walked to the snack bar and Collin bought us gummy bears, popcorn, chocolate, cheese nachos, and two bottles of water.

"Who's going to eat all of this?" I asked him amused.

"We are." He said seriously and I looked at him disbelievingly.

He didn't even give me a chance to say anything as he placed his arm around my waist and started walking towards the auditorium that was screening the movie we had chosen to watch, as Rosalinda followed.

The movie had just started so we sat down quickly. Collin handed Rosalinda a bag of popcorn and held the other one for me and him to share. He placed his arm around my shoulder; pulling me closer to him and I laid my head on his chest. I took a handful of the popcorn and popped it in my mouth. Collin was busy placing kisses on my neck making me squirm and giggle. I turned my head to look at Rosalinda and noticed that she was too engrossed in the movie to notice anyone or anything around her.

"Collin." I whispered. "My sister's here."

He groaned then placed one last kiss on the side of my head. He tightened his hold on me and I snuggled even closer to him and unconsciously drew circles on his chest. Collin suddenly held my hand; stopping me. I looked up at him with a questioning look on my face, but he didn't need to say anything. The expression on his face said it all; he was turned on. I had turned him on. Thank god it was dark inside the auditorium because I felt my face turning red so I hid my face in his chest.

"I like you, Esmeralda." He whispered huskily in my ear.

I looked up at him with a smile on my face. "I like you too." My tone matched his.

"No, I like you, Esmeralda." He repeated. "I want you to be mine." He then clarified.

I looked at him shocked and surprisingly happy. I liked Collin. I would be lying if I said otherwise. He was different from all the men that came to the strip club. He treated me as a human being with feelings and not just as a stripper that stripped every night for dirty, old men.

"Esmeralda?"

I blinked twice and looked at him. "Yes?"

"I want you to be mine, Esmeralda." His voice was tender and rough.

"I want that too." I told him in a heartbeat.

His lips turned upwards in a smile. He said nothing and just pulled me to his chest and kissed the top of my head. I stayed snuggled against his chest; listening to his heartbeat.

"The movie was great!" Rosalinda exclaimed once we walked out of the auditorium. "Did you like it, Es?" She asked me excitedly.

I looked up at Collin who had a smirk on his face then looked back at Rosalinda. "Yes, it was great." I lied.

I didn't even know what the movie was about. After Collin told me that he wanted me to be his, I wasn't able to concentrate on anything else.

"Where do you want to go next?" Collin asked us as we walked out to the parking lot.

"We could just go home." I suggested half heartedly. I wanted to spend every second with him.

Collin appeared to be thinking as he unlocked his car and we got in. "One more stop first." He said.

About fifteen minutes later, the car came to halt in front of a café; a rather elegant looking one I might add. We stepped out of the car, Rosalinda came and stood by my side and we watched as Collin handed his car keys to one of the valet parking men before we walked inside the café. The café was crowded, but fortunately there was one empty table.

"What would you like to order?" The waitress asked us.

"Three hot chocolates" Collin answered for us then looked at us. "Do you want something to go along with it?" He asked us and both Rosalinda and I shook our heads no. "They make the best hot chocolate you'll ever taste." Collin said once the waitress left. "You do like hot chocolate, right?" He looked at me and then at Rosalinda. I scrunched up my nose in fake disgust and Collin's eyes went wide. "I should've asked. We could order something else if you want." He sounded apologetic.

I giggled. "I'm just messing with you." I told him still smiling.

"What about you, Rosa? I can call you Rosa, right?" He asked my sister as I looked at him with the upmost admiration.

"Yes." She nodded. "I love hot chocolate and you can call me Rosa."

Collin nodded with a smile on his face then looked at me, but the smile was gone and there was a smirk there instead. I suddenly felt his hand on my thigh and he squeezed gently.

A little while later, the waitress served us our hot chocolate with a couple of marshmallows on the side.

"Try it." Collin urged both Rosalinda and I.

Rosalinda took a sip first then placed the cup back on the table before saying. "It's the best!" She smiled at me. "It really is the best!" She gushed.

"Let's see." I said with uncertainty before placing the cup of hot chocolate to my lips. The taste instantly sent me to heaven. I closed my eyes and moaned in sheer happiness. "This is amazing." I admitted as I opened my eyes. Collin was looking at me with dark eyes while Rosalinda was just giggling.

Collin held out one marshmallow for me to taste. "Try this."

I munched on the marshmallow even though I wasn't a huge fan of them, but it tasted really good alongside the hot chocolate.

We sat for a short while until Rosalinda said she was tired and would like to go home. I knew that she had exerted herself today with the ice skating and she needed to rest. Minutes later, Collin paid the bill and we exited the café.

"Is Rosa okay?" Collin asked me in a hushed tone as he looked at her from the rearview mirror.

I turned my body sideways in my seat and looked at my sister that was looking rather pale. Even the makeup that she had on did nothing.

"Are you okay, sweetie?" I asked her.

"Yes, I'm just tired." She said.

I looked back at Collin. "How much longer till we arrive back home?" I asked him worriedly.

"Just a few more minutes" He replied.

I nodded and looked back at my sister again. She gave me a reassuring smile. She was a strong girl alright.

Just like Collin said, a few minutes later we arrived at our house. I was the first to step out the car followed by Rosalinda and then Collin.

Rosalinda gave Collin a small tired smile and thanked him. "Thank you for today. I had a really great time, and I'm sorry that I ruined what was supposed to be a date."

"You didn't ruin anything. You are welcome to go out with us whenever you feel like it, okay?" Collin said firmly and Rosalinda nodded with a small smile. "It was a pleasure meeting you, Rosa."

"Likewise" She said.

I looked at my sister with a small smile. "Go in, sweetie, I'll follow you in a minute." She nodded and started walking inside the house.

I watched her as she closed the door behind her before looking back at Collin.

"Thank you for being nice to her." I told him.

He wrapped his arms around my waist and pulled me closer to him. "You don't have to thank me, baby. Your family is my family."

I wrapped my arms around Collin's neck and placed my lips on his. He licked my bottom lip then suckled gently. I eagerly parted my lips for him. He plunged his tongue inside, dominated my mouth, and stroked it to ecstasy. I pulled back for air, but Collin didn't stop. He started kissing down my neck and I tilted my head sideways to give him more access as I tried to catch my breath.

"Collin, stop." I giggled as I grabbed a fistful of his hair and pulled his head back. "We're on the street." I told him.

"Who cares?" He asked annoyed. "You're my girlfriend." His arms were still around my waist so he pulled me even closer to him if that was even possible.

"Yeah, I am." I told him with a wide smile.

"Yeah, you are." He said in a low voice as he once again reclaimed my lips in another kiss. I giggled into the kiss making him pull back. "You're ruining the moment." He said sternly.

"I'm sorry." I told him with a smile even though I was anything but apologetic. "I have to go inside now."

"Okay." He nodded half heartedly.

I grabbed his face with both of my hands and pressed my lips to his in a quick kiss. "Goodnight."

He released his arms from around my waist and pressed a kiss on my cheeks. "Goodnight, baby"

**********Remember to vote, comment, share, recommend, add 'Trixie' to your reading list, and follow. :)

Chapter 8 - Strip Club Brawl

The music started playing and my body moved on its own accord as I looked at Collin. Everyone in the strip club had gone blurry in my eyes; all I could see was Collin, and only Collin.

It was like I was giving him a private dance just for his eyes.

I swayed my hips from side to side and bent down sexily and erotically before coming back up. I squeezed my boobs then released my hands and raised them up before letting them trace the sides of my body. My eyes never once left Collin's and I knew he was turned on which made me want to go on; it made me want to please him. I turned around and bent down so that my bottom was up in the air and wiggled my butt.

I was brought back to reality when I felt someone squeeze my bottom. I quickly stood up and looked at the man with narrowed eyes. There was absolutely no touching allowed in the strip club.

The clients had one important rule to follow; you see, but you don't touch. However, they had a problem following that rule.

My gaze went to Collin and apparently that squeeze hadn't gone unnoticed by him since he was glaring at the back of the man's head. I continued dancing like nothing had happened, but unfortunately I felt another squeeze on my butt. I turned around and noticed that it was the same man from before.

"No touching boys!" I wiggled my finger with a seductive smile on my face even though I was annoyed.

The man just smirked triumphantly. Thank god Collin couldn't see his expression because I could see that he had his fists clenched by his sides and he was ready to fight. I looked at him with pleading eyes, not wanting him to start anything.

My hands went to the straps of my bra and I ran my fingers through it slowly in a teasing manner.

"Show us the goodies, hot stuff." The same man yelled, and I could tell that he was drunk from the way he slurred on his words.

Before I could even blink, the man was on the floor with Collin on top of him punching the living daylights out of him. I could see that the man was unconscious beneath him, but that didn't stop Collin as he threw hit after hit to the bloodied man. No one tried to help break up the fight as they all stood at the side watching the scene unfold in front of them.

"Collin, Stop!" I screamed in panic as I jumped off the stage and went to his side. I grabbed his hand in an attempt to stop him, but he just wouldn't. "Collin, please stop." I was pleading, no begging.

The man was unconscious with blood all over his face. I was scared that Collin would actually kill him.

Fortunately, Collin noticed my panicked state and stopped punching the guy then looked at me; his eyes softening. Before either of us could say anything, security came over and started walking Collin out.

"Don't touch me!" Collin warned the guards angrily as he shrugged off their hands. "I can walk myself out." He looked at me, but my stare was blank. I was still trying to make sense of what had just happened. He then quietly walked out of the strip club.

I looked at the unconscious man that was being held by paramedics then saw Conner walking towards me.

"My office, now!" He ordered in a harsh whisper.

I didn't reply nor care about him as I walked out of the strip club in nothing but my stripper costume. I saw Collin standing outside the strip club running his hand through his hair. He suddenly looked up as if noticing my presence.

"What was that all about?" I yelled angrily as I walked up to him.

"He was touching you and saying some nasty things!" He retorted. "Do you want me to stand by and watch him sexually harass my girlfriend?"

"This is my job!" I yelled and laughed humorlessly. "Take it or leave it! Being a stripper puts me in such positions."

"I can't handle seeing other men treat you like trash."

"Then leave!" I retorted angrily. "I don't need drama in my life or my job, Collin. If you can't handle it then please just leave before things go any further between us."

"I will never leave you!" He stated with anger and possessiveness in his tone.

I sighed and ran my hand through my hair. "Go home, Collin." I waved him off. "We'll talk later."

"I'm not leaving without you." He said with so much determination in his voice.

"I'm not leaving, Collin. I have a job to get back to." I said. "If I still have a job, that is." I muttered quietly and tiredly. "Just go home."

Fortunately, Collin didn't put up a fight, but he didn't leave. He just stood there and watched me as I walked back in to the strip club.

The first thing I noticed was that the strip club inside was back to normal. There were a couple of strippers on stage, but Conner was nowhere in sight. I figured he would be in his office so I walked there and knocked on the door.

"Come in." I turned the knob and opened the door then walked in. "Close the door." He said as he looked at me through narrowed eyes. I closed the door and stood in front of his desk.

"You wanted to see me?" I asked.

"What was that, Trixie? You know better than to bring your personal life here." He said; his tone was calm, not in a good way though. "This is bad for business."

"You think I don't know that?" I asked him.

"Then get your life in track. I don't need shit like this happening in my strip club."

"Don't worry, it won't be happening again." I told him. I was trying as much as I could to control my anger.

"Good. You're one of my best dancers here and I would hate to lose you." He said more softly this time. I nodded firmly, but didn't say anything. "You could go back to work now." I nodded once more before walking out of his office.

#

"Have a good night, Trixie." Joe told me as he opened the taxi door for me.

I gave him a thankful smile then stepped inside the taxi. I still couldn't believe what had happened and I was still trying to wrap my head around it.

The taxi suddenly came to a halt in front of my house. I paid the taxi driver and stepped out. As soon as I looked up, I saw Collin standing at my front door. I sighed and walked up to him.

"What do you want, Collin?" I asked him tiredly as I opened my purse and brought out the house key. "I'm tired and I want to sleep."

"I'm not sorry for what I did." He said.

I looked up at him in disbelief. "I will not stand by and let men ogle you and grope you and call you names. I'm sorry, but I can't do that."

"For the millionth time Collin, this is my job!"

"Then quit!" He retorted angrily.

"Quit?" I scoffed. "Collin, please go home. I am tired and I want to sleep." I repeated, not wanting to get into a fight with him in the wee hours of the morning.

"Yes, quit. Is it money you want? I'll give you money. I'll give you anything you want, but please quit." He pleaded with his eyes.

I sighed and rubbed my eyes with the palm of my hands.

I suddenly felt both of his hands on my shoulder. "Why won't you quit, Es?"

I looked up at him. He had a sad and defeated look in his eyes. Should I tell him about Rosalinda's cancer? No you shouldn't my mind told me.If Rosalinda knew that I told him, she wouldn't be happy with me.

"I already told you Collin, I need the money." He was about to say something when I stopped him. "You knew what you were going to get yourself into when you said you wanted me to be yours. You knew that I was a stripper." Collin released his hand from my arm and stared at me with a defeated look on his face. "Collin, I'm tired and I need to rest. We'll talk later."

I didn't give him a chance to say anything as I unlocked the door and walked in. I rested my back against the door and sighed deeply then walked to the window beside the door and peeked outside through the curtains. I saw him still standing where I had left him. All I wanted to do at that moment was hug him, but I knew I shouldn't.

He stayed there for a couple of minutes before he stepped inside his car and drove away.

I walked to my room and closed the door behind me. I walked to the bathroom and stripped off my clothes and threw them in the hamper. I took a quick shower since I was tired then flopped down on my bed.

As much as I was tired and as much as I was fighting my eyes to stay open, I couldn't help but think about Collin. Was I too hard on him? Did I treat him harshly even though all he was being was a caring and loving boyfriend?

I internally groaned and grabbed my phone from the nightstand. I pressed his number and was about to hit the send button when I noticed the time; it was late. I decided I would call him first thing the next morning. I needed to apologize. I needed to let him know that even though I see where he was coming from that it was not okay for him to hit whoever looked my way.

I placed my phone back on the nightstand and grabbed the duvet; snuggling under it. I closed my eyes and willed my thoughts to go away. I just wanted to sleep and not think about anything. Luckily, it didn't take me long until I fell into deep sleep.

**********Remember to vote, comment, share, recommend, add 'Trixie' to your reading list, and follow. :)

Chapter 9 - Apologies

I woke up startled to the sound of banging on the front door. My heart started beating fast and my palms became sweaty. I grabbed my pillow then carefully and quietly walked out of my room. I stood against the door and said in a strong voice; well as strong as I could manage.

"I'm calling the police!"

"Es, let me in."

I instantly recognized Collin's voice and let out a breath that I didn't know I was holding.

I opened the door and he looked at me then his gaze went to my pillow.

"A pillow?" he chuckled. "Couldn't you find anything softer?" He said his voice dripping of sarcasm.

"Ha ha" I said grumpily and walked to the living room. I knew Collin was on my heels.

I sat down on the couch and hugged the pillow to my chest. "What do you want, Collin?" I asked him. "It's still too early."

"I know. I'm sorry. I couldn't sleep." He said; still standing up.

"How is that my problem?" I asked him in disbelief. "You didn't need to ruin my sleep."

He came towards me and sat down on the couch beside me.

"Well, you were the reason that I couldn't sleep." He said. "I couldn't handle the fact that you were mad at me." I didn't reply and just looked away. "Es, please say something."

"I need coffee." Was the only thing I said as I placed the pillow to the side and stood up.

I walked to the kitchen and opened the cupboard. I brought out two mugs and poured coffee into them then held them in my hands and walked back out to the living room. I placed one mug in front of Collin on the coffee table, but kept holding the other one as I sat back down at the same spot. I took a sip of my coffee and looked at Collin who was watching me intently.

"I'm not mad at you." I told him as I held the coffee mug in my hand.

"You're not?" He asked; his eyes lighting up.

I shook my head. "I'm not mad at you. I know that you did what you did because you care about me." He was about to say something when I raised my hand; stopping him. "Let me continue, Collin." He nodded sadly. "It doesn't mean that it's okay for you to do what you did. It is not acceptable. One more punch and you would have killed the guy." I paused a little and looked at his sad expressions before continuing. "I could have lost my job because of what you did. I do not need such drama, not in my personal life and definitely not in my job."

"I couldn't handle myself. The way he was groping you and talking to you. I just... I lost it."

I sighed. "Collin, you have to control yourself. You can't lose it every time someone looks my way or talks to me. I'm a stripper, I'm going to get groped whether I like it or not."

"I don't understand why you won't quit your job." He said as he looked at me.

"You don't need to understand, Collin. You just have to accept me the way I am." Collin was quiet for a moment. He had his eyebrows furrowed like he was thinking about something. "Maybe we rushed into this relationship. Let's just stay friends for now and see where it takes us."

Collin looked at me with narrowed eyes, and if he was a cartoon character, steam would be coming out of his ears.

"Is that what you want?" He asked me calmly; too calmly. I could tell he was trying to control his anger.

"No." I shook my head. "It's not what I want, Collin, but it feels like it's the right choice. I'd rather keep you in my life as a friend than lose you completely, which is something that will happen at some point if you keep having problems with what I do for a living."

"No, it's not the right choice. It's not even an option." Collin shook his head then scooted closer towards me. He held my hands and looked straight into my eyes. "I like you, Es. I'll try to control my anger, but I can't promise you anything." I could tell that he was being sincere.

I nodded. "Okay." I figured that it was the best he could give me at that moment, and I had to admit that I didn't want to lose him.

"Okay?" He asked me with a hopeful smile. "So we're okay?"

I nodded as a small smile made its way to my face. "We're okay." I whispered.

I brought the cup of coffee to my mouth and took a sip then spit it back into the cup. "I hate cold coffee." I grumbled.

Collin took the mug from my hands and placed it on the table. "Go change. I'm taking you out for breakfast."

"Don't you have work?" I suddenly realized that he should have been at work and not here.

"I'm the boss, baby." He boasted with a grin.

I stood up from my seat, grabbed my pillow, and walked to my room. I placed the pillow back on the bed then opened my closet and grabbed a white skirt and a blush colored top. I stripped off my pyjamas and put the clothes on then slipped on my nude heels. I ran the brush through my hair then grabbed my purse and cell phone, and walked out of the room.

Collin stood up from his seat and looked at me with so much admiration in his eyes.

"Ready?" He asked me, and I nodded. He walked towards me and grabbed my hand then placed a kiss there. "You look beautiful, baby." He complimented.

"Thank you." I said as I started to blush.

"Where are Rosa and your mom?" He asked me as we walked towards his car.

"Mom is at work, and Rosa is at school."

"Is there anywhere you'd like to go?" Collin looked at me sideways as soon as we stepped inside the car.

I shook my head. "You choose." He nodded then told his driver where to take us.

He then gave me a heartwarming smile and intertwined our hands together. He raised it up and placed a kiss there then placed it on my lap.

About thirty minutes later, we arrived at a fancy looking café. I was glad that I had chosen something nice to wear rather than just jeans and a top. The hostess seated us at a small table beside the window. She handed us two menus then left.

"Have you chosen?" Collin asked me and I nodded. He gestured for the waitress to come.

"Have you decided on your order?" she asked us with a smile.

"Yes." Collin answered formally. "Es?"

"I'll have the fruit salad, Greek yogurt, granola, and a cup of orange juice, please."

The waitress nodded and jotted my order down then looked at Collin.

"I'll have the poached eggs on sourdough with salmon." The waitress nodded and jotted down his order as well. "I'll also have orange juice."

The waitress nodded and grabbed our menus then walked away.

"Do you have something planned for today, baby?" Collin asked me once the waitress was out of sight.

"Well, I was planning on sleeping all day, but my plan got ruined." I gave him a teasing smile.

"Do you want me to drop you off home?" He asked me seriously.

I chuckled, shook my head, and grabbed his hand that rested on the table. "I prefer being here." I gave him a small smile then added. "With you"

His lips turned upwards in a smile. He was about to say something when the waitress appeared with our plates. I released my hand from his and she placed our plates on the table. I didn't know I was starving until I saw the delicious looking plates that made my stomach growl in hunger.

"Can I steal some of yours?" I asked Collin. His plate looked really tasty.

"Only if you let me steal some of yours" He retorted.

I nodded with a grin then picked up my fork and leaned forward and ate a bit of his poached egg and salmon. It tasted really good. Collin then picked up his spoon and leaned forward as well as he stole some of my fruit salad and yogurt.

"That was really delicious." I stated as I pushed my empty plate away.

"I'm sure you're more delicious." Collin complimented me.

The hidden meaning in his sentence made my cheeks blush. He leaned forward in his chair and placed a chaste kiss on my lips.

"You look beautiful when you blush." That made my cheeks heat up even more. "Are you ready to leave?" He asked me.

I nodded. "Yes, I just need to use the restroom first."

"Take your time, baby."

I gave him a small smile and stood up from my seat then walked to the bathroom making sure to sway my hips more than necessary. I wanted to tease him. He was teasing me without even knowing it just by the way he looked.

I pushed the bathroom door open and washed my hands then dried them off before walking back out. Collin was paying the bill when I arrived at the table.

"Ready?" He asked me and I nodded then grabbed my purse. He stood up from his seat and came to my side and snaked his arm around my waist; pulling me to him. "You're getting payback for what you did." He whispered mischievously in my ear.

"What did I do?" I asked him feigning innocence and ignorance. I knew very well what he meant. I knew very well that I had turned him on exactly like I had planned to.

"You know very well what you did, miss enchantress." He looked sideways at me and gave me a teasing smile.

Collin's cell phone rang as soon as we settled ourselves inside his car. He brought his phone out of his pocket and looked at the caller ID before placing the phone to his ear.

"Yes, Lila?" He answered his phone. "Okay." He sighed. "I'll be in the office shortly." He ended the call and placed it back in his pocket then turned to look at me. "I'm sorry, baby."

**********Remember to vote, comment, share, recommend, add 'Trixie' to your reading list, and follow. :)

Chapter 10 - The Office

"I'm sorry, baby." Collin must have noticed the confused look on my face because he added. "This was my personal assistant informing me about a Skype meeting that I had forgotten about."

"Oh. Well, could you drop me home first?" I asked him.

He stared at me for a moment as if thinking about something. "Would you like to come with me?"

"To your meeting?" I asked him with a raised eyebrow.

"No, baby, to the office" He said. Collin could see me hesitating. "You're coming." He added firmly; not letting me say anything then told his driver to takes us to the headquarters. I shook my head and smiled amusedly.

I could feel that Collin was nervous for some reason as the driver drove us to our destination.

"Why are you nervous?"

He looked sideways at me. "This conference call is with a potential client that I have been trying to win over for quite some."

"Oh." I nodded "I'm sure it will be okay." I assured him, but all I got was a silent nod.

I looked out the window then suddenly felt Collin's hand on mine as he raised it and pressed a kiss there. I leaned forward in my seat and kissed his cheek.

A short while later, we approached a huge twenty-story glass building with Edwards Inc written in steel over the glass front doors. The driver stopped the car in front of the building then stepped out and opened Collin's door before opening mine. I looked up at the intimidating looking building then suddenly felt an arm around my waist. I looked sideways at Collin who had a smile on his face.

Collin started leading me inside the building. I could feel everyone's eyes on us, but Collin paid attention to no one and just kept walking towards the elevator. I lowered my head; feeling uncomfortable. Collin pressed the elevator button and we waited for it to arrive. Luckily, when the elevator doors opened, it was empty. We stepped inside and Collin pressed the 20th floor button.

"Why is everyone staring at us like that?" I asked him once the elevator doors closed.

Collin smirked then pushed me softly against the elevator wall and placed his hands on either side of my head. "I have never brought any woman here." He told me in a low and husky voice.

"Never?" I asked him in disbelief.

"Never, baby. You are the first." He placed a kiss beneath my earlobe. "And the last" He whispered in my ear as he continued nibbling that sweet and ticklish spot.

My hands wrapped around his neck and I tugged on his hair. I leaned my head to the side, giving him more access to my neck and he placed kisses all over. My breathing was becoming hard. I was feeling pressure on my neck and pressure down there.

Just then the elevator binged and the doors opened. Before I could even blink, Collin had pushed himself away from me and his hand found mine as he intertwined them and started walking out of the elevator.

My legs were shaky and I could barely hold myself together.

"Isn't payback sweet?" He whispered in my ear then chuckled lowly.

That wicked man, he did it on purpose.

We kept walking towards what I assumed was his office. He opened the door and we walked in.

"This is my office." He said.

The office was spacious with the color theme being grey and white. It had glass windows that overlooked the city. The view was breathtaking. Collin released his hold on my hand and I walked towards the window and just stood there and looked outside.

"This is simply breathtaking." I said still looking out the window.

"Yes, it is." He said.

I felt him wrap his arms around me from behind as he rested his head on the top of my shoulder. I looked sideways at him and he gave me a heartwarming smile.

A knock was suddenly heard on the door. Collin pulled away from me.

"Come in."

A young beautiful lady walked in with a beige folder in her hand. She placed the folder on his desk then just stood there and wrung her hands nervously. I gave Collin a questioning look, but he just looked unfazed.

"Your conference meeting is in about ten minutes, Mr. Collins." She finally said courteously then kept standing in her spot as if wanting to say something else yet afraid.

"Is there something else, Lila?"

"Mr. Fernandez asked about you, I told him you were out of the office today." She rushed out as she glanced up at him for a mere second before lowering down her gaze.

"Okay, Lila." He nodded. "If anyone else asks about me, you tell them the same thing because I'm leaving right after the meeting." Lila nodded. "You may leave." She nodded thankfully and practically scurried away.

"What was that about?" I asked him as soon as I heard the door close shut.

Collin walked towards his desk chair and sat down. "What was what?" He asked me as he turned on his computer.

"Why does Lila seem scared of you?"

"Come here." He ordered softly and patted his lap. I walked towards him and sat down on his lap. "Lila is new here so she has probably heard what they say about me around the office."

"What do they say?" I asked him suddenly feeling intrigued.

"That I'm ruthless, cruel, harsh to name a few."

I looked at him with wide eyes. "You don't care that they say those things about you?"

"I am what they say, baby." I gave him a questioning look. He hadn't been all of those things with me. "You have to be all of those things in order to be a good businessman." He explained.

His Skype suddenly started ringing. I knew that this was his potential client calling so I stood up and sat on one of the couches so that I wouldn't appear in the video call.

It was about an hour and a half later and I was getting bored. God, how long does a meeting take? I stood up from my seat and started walking around the office. I noticed how he didn't have anything personal like a family photo or something.

"What are you looking for?" Collin's voice startled me. I turned around and found him standing behind me.

"How come you don't have any photos of your family?"

"I like to keep my personal life and work life separate." I nodded and started walking back to the couch then sat down.

"Are you done?" I asked him and he nodded with a grin.

"You're my good luck charm, baby." He said as he sat down beside me and pulled me closer to him.

"Mm... Why is that?"

"I just won a million dollar account." My eyes went wide as saucers. Million dollars! That was a lot of money.

Collin captured my lips hungrily and passionately. I parted my lips and he slipped his tongue inside my mouth in a sweet invasion. He tasted sweeter than Godiva chocolate. I could get drunk on his sweet nectar. His hands lingered on my breast for a moment before it started moving down there. His hands found my sweet spot and he started rubbing me to ecstasy. I pulled back from the kiss as I started breathing hard. Collin start rubbing faster and faster and I raised my hips higher as I started feeling my orgasm getting closer. He started kissing down my neck and that's when I screamed his name and flopped back down. I rested my head on Collin's chest as I tried to control my breath.

Before either of us could say anything, my phone started ringing. Collin handed me my bag from beside him and I brought my phone out.

"Hello?" I answered breathlessly without checking who was calling.

"Why do you sound like you've just ran a marathon?" Rosalinda asked.

I chuckled nervously. "Is something wrong?" I asked her; changing the subject.

"Well, I came back from school and you weren't home." She sounded disappointed. "Aren't you coming home to have lunch with us?"

I looked at Collin who was looking at me with adoration in his eyes. "I'm with Collin, sweetie."

I heard my mom's voice on the other side of the phone, but I couldn't figure out what she was saying. "Mom says that you should bring Collin home to have lunch with us as well." Rosalinda said.

I placed my hand on the speaker and looked at Collin. "Do you want to have lunch at my house?" Collin's lips turned upwards in a grin and he nodded. I removed my hand from the speaker. "We'll be there shortly, Rosa."

"Okay." She sounded happy. "We'll be waiting for you."

I hung up the phone and looked sideways at Collin. "That was... amazing." I said; not finding a better word. My head was jumbled.

He kissed the side of my head. "I love it when you scream my name." He said making my cheeks heat up and I looked away.

He placed his hand under my chin and turned my face back to look at him.

"There's nothing to be ashamed of, Es. You'll be screaming my name a lot more." He promised with a smirk.

I grabbed my bag and quickly stood up.

"My mom and sister are waiting for us."

Collin chuckled then stood up. "Let's go then." He said.

He placed his arm around my waist and we walked out of his office. Lila, Collin's personal assistant, looked up at us, but then quickly looked away. I felt sorry for the poor girl.

Collin's driver was waiting for us in front of the building. We stepped inside the car, and Collin ordered his driver to take us back to my house.

**********Remember to vote, comment, share, recommend, add 'Trixie' to your reading list, and follow. :)

Chapter 11 - Meeting the Parents

I opened the front door and walked in with Collin on my heels. We entered the living room where we found Rosalinda sprawled on the couch watching TV.

"Don't you have homework, Rosa?" I asked my sister.

She turned around and looked up at me then ran towards me and hugged me. Pulling back, she looked at Collin and greeted him with a shy smile before looking back at me.

"I do, but I was waiting for you to help me. There's this lesson in geometry that I don't understand."

"Geometry is not my strongest point, sweetie, but I'll try to help you."

"You know." Collin piped up. "I'm very good at geometry. I could help you if you want to." He offered.

"Really?" Rosalinda asked him with a smile and Collin nodded. "Okay, I'll just go get my books and I'll be right back." She started walking towards her room when I stopped her.

"Where's mom?"

"She's in the kitchen cooking lunch." She said then turned back around and continued walking to her room.

I turned to Collin and placed my hand on his chest. "I'll be right back, babe." I kissed his cheek and walked to the kitchen where mom was standing by the stove stirring something in the pot.

"Do you need help, mom?" I asked her.

She turned around and a smile made its way to her face. "You're here."

"Yes, Collin and I just arrived."

She nodded happily. "Can you help me mix the salad?"

"Of course"

Mom and I prepared the table then I went in to the living room to inform Collin and Rosalinda that lunch was ready. Collin was explaining something to Rosalinda and I waited for him to finish before I spoke.

"Lunch is ready." Rosalinda looked at Collin who told her that they'll continue after lunch before she stood up and walked past me to the dining room. I walked towards Collin and sat down on his lap.

"Thank you, babe"

"For what?" He asked me confused.

"For being you" I placed a chaste kiss on his lips then stood up and held out my hand for him to take then we both walked to the dining room.

After we finished lunch, Collin and Rosalinda retired back to the living room to finish Rosalinda's homework, while I stayed back with my mom and helped her with the dishes.

"Collin is a good guy." She said as she handed me a plate to dry.

"Yes, he is." I smiled as I thought about him.

"You never told me how you two met."

My eyes went wide as saucers and I froze in my spot. Mom turned to look at me and I quickly said. "We met at work." Well, it wasn't a complete lie.

We finished the dishes then joined both Rosalinda and Collin in the living room. Rosalinda was writing something on her notebook, but Collin noticed me and looked up at me with a smile. I sat down beside him on the couch while mom sat opposite of us on the arm-chair.

"Are you done?" I asked him.

"Almost" He replied.

We stayed for a little while longer before Collin stood up to leave. He looked at me. "Are you ready to go?"

"I'm going with you?" I asked him dumbfounded.

Collin chuckled, and I could see Rosalinda and mom from the corner of my eyes smiling.

"I want to take you somewhere, baby."

I nodded and stood up. Collin held my hand in his and we said our goodbyes before walking out.

I watched as Collin exchanged a few hushed words with his driver before we got inside the car.

"Where are you taking me?" I asked him.

"To my parents' house" Collin answered as he typed away on his phone.

"You're telling me this now?" I practically screamed.

Collin looked up from his phone and noticed the panicked expression on my face. He tucked his phone into his pocket and held my hands.

"Baby, everything's going to be okay."

"Yes sure. I mean what parent wouldn't want their son to be with a stripper." My tone was dripping with sarcasm. "Oh hi, ma'am, I'm stripper what about you?" I said in a mock tone as I held out my hand as if shaking an imaginary person.

"Es, Es, look at me." Collin tightened his hold on my hands. I looked up at him and he had a small smile on his face. "Didn't you ask me in the office why I didn't have personal photos?" I nodded wordlessly. "I want to show you the real me, baby."

"You should've told me. Now, your parents will think I'm a gold digging whore."

I could see him clenching his jaw. "You are not a gold digging whore, do you understand?" He asked me in a terrifyingly calm tone. I nodded meekly. "I didn't tell you because I knew this were the way you would react. My parents will love you I can assure you that; no matter what your profession is. However, if you're not comfortable about telling them that you're a stripper, we can skip that piece of information for now. Okay?"

"Okay." I agreed in a low voice.

"Chin up, beautiful." He placed a kiss on my lips.

Shortly after, the car came to a stop in front of a beautiful mansion with a water fountain in the middle that was surrounded by pink flowers.

"You live here?" I asked him in disbelief.

"I used to live here, baby. Now I have my own penthouse."

I didn't have time to say anything as the driver opened Collin's door and he stepped out before coming over to my side and opening my door. We walked towards the front door and Collin rang the doorbell. A moment later, the maid opened the door and let us in. She led us to the garden where Collin's parents were at.

"Silas, look who's here." A middle aged woman said in an excited tone to the man beside her then stood up and walked towards us with a huge smile on her face. She pulled Collin into a hug then pulled back and looked at me; the smile not wavering. "Who is this pretty lady?"

"Esmeralda." I told her with a wide smile.

"She's my girlfriend, mom, so be nice." Collin warned with a playful smile.

Collin's mother turned sideways. "Silas, would you come here already?" She waved at her husband then turned back around to look at me. "It's nice to meet you, sweetheart. I'm Margaret." She said with a smile.

"It's nice to meet you too, Mrs. Edwards."

"Oh, nonsense" her husband came to stand beside her. "You will call us Silas and Margaret." He said.

"Yes." His wife agreed. "Now come and have a seat." She said as she pulled me from Collin's hold then yelled for the maid to come.

I turned around and looked at Collin who was trying to stifle a laugh.

We sat in the garden for what seemed like a long time just talking. It didn't feel like I was meeting my boyfriend's parents, but rather old friends. I felt comfortable around those people.

"Collin is here?" We heard a voice ask, and then a man that looked in his mid twenties appeared. "And who is this beautiful lady?" He looked at me with a flirtatious smile.

"She's mine, Ben. Back off." Collin warned.

Ben raised his arms in surrender. "Hold your horses, brother. I just wanted to know who she is."

"I'm Esmeralda." I outstretched my hand.

Ben took my hand and kissed it. "I'm Ben, and if you ever decide to leave my brother, I'll be waiting."

"Benjamin Edwards! Watch your tongue!" Collin warned as he pulled me to his side and I chuckled at his possessive action.

Benjamin laughed. "Oh, please. You know I'm just joking with you."

"You better be." He warned in a dangerous tone.

"You must be a very special girl, Esmeralda." Benjamin told me. "Collin has never been so possessive about any girl before." I smiled shyly and leaned more into Collin.

Margaret insisted that we stay for dinner, and Collin and I agreed. I don't know what time it was until we decided to leave. Margaret, Silas, and Benjamin walked us to the door.

"It was very nice meeting you, Esmeralda. Please do come again."

I gave Margaret a wide smile. "I would love to, if Collin brings me again." I looked up at Collin lovingly.

"If he doesn't, give me a call" Benjamin said. "I'll take you wherever you want."

Collin glared at Benjamin who just gave him a boyish grin.

"Come on, tough guy, let's go." I said as I patted his chest, making his parents laugh. We said our goodbyes then left.

As soon as we settled ourselves inside the car, I couldn't stop gushing about how nice his parents were and he couldn't help but point out that he told me so.

I pulled out my phone from my purse and noticed that it was quarter to ten. "Baby, Can you drop me off to work?"

"Do I have to?" He asked me seriously.

I scooted closer to him and kissed his lips. "Yes, please."

Collin ordered his driver to drive us to the strip club. As soon as we arrived, Collin opened the car door and was about to step out when I grabbed his arm.

"Where do you think you're going?" I asked him with a raised eyebrow.

"I'm going in with you."

"No, you're not."

"Don't argue with me, Es."

I scooted closer to him and straddled his lap. Collin pressed a button and a black screen appeared; separating us from his driver.

"I don't need babysitting, Collin." I told him softly.

"I just want to make sure you're okay."

"We have bodyguards in there to make sure of that." Collin sighed and rubbed his temples. "I'll be okay, baby. I promise."

"Okay, do you want me to pick you up at least?"

"No, it's fine. I'll take a taxi." I could see Collin trying to think so I kissed his lips distracting him.

"You will call me as soon as you step foot inside your house. Okay?" He ordered sternly once he pulled back.

"Yes, sir" I mock saluted him and he rolled his eyes making me giggle. I then placed a soft kiss on his lips. "I'll call you later, handsome." I opened the door and walked inside the strip club.

#

I opened the door to my house as quietly as I could and slipped inside then walked to my bedroom and closed the door.

I sat down on my bed and brought out my phone from my purse then called Collin. He answered on the first ring.

"Are you home?" He asked me worriedly.

I chuckled. "Yes, babe, I just arrived." I rubbed my forehead. "I'm tired and I need to take a shower."

"Okay I'll let you go now." I nodded even though he couldn't see me then we both hung up.

Once I finished my shower I flopped down on my bed. Fatigue washed over me like a wave, making me tired down to my bones. I closed my eyes wanting to sleep when I heard my phone vibrate. I picked it up and noticed that I had a new text message from Collin.

'Goodnight, beautiful xx'

A smile made its way to my face in spite of my tired state as I typed my reply.

'Goodnight, handsome. Xoxo'

**********Remember to vote, comment, share, recommend, add 'Trixie' to your reading list, and follow. :)

Chapter 12 - Unwanted Visit

I woke up the next morning to an empty house. After eating breakfast and cleaning up a bit, I decided to prepare lunch.

I opened the fridge and stood there; trying to decide what I wanted to make until I decided on lasagna and onion soup. I knew those were my mom and my sister's favorite. However, I noticed that we didn't have the needed ingredients so I walked back to my room, put on a top and a shirt, shoved some money in my pocket before walking out of the house.

#

"That will be thirty five dollars." The young woman at the register told me.

I nodded and handed her a pile of singles that I had made last night. The young woman looked at the money and then back at me, but didn't comment. She counted the money before placing it in the register then handed me the plastic bag.

I thanked her and walked out of the grocery store then started to make my way back home.

"Es" I heard an overly familiar voice as I was opening the front door of the house.

No, it couldn't be him I thought to myself. I turned around and my suspicions were proven right.

"What are you doing here?" I asked my estranged father in a cold tone.

"I came to see my family." He said in a soft tone as he walked closer towards me.

"Family?" I scoffed. "You lost the right to call us your family the moment you bailed on us."

"Es, please you have to put yourself in my position. What would you have done?"

"I was in your position, and so was mom." I laughed humorlessly. "And guess what? We stuck around."

"Can we talk inside?" He asked as he started looking around.

"No." I answered in a clipped tone. "We have nothing to talk about."

"Es, please don't be harsh on me. Just give me a second chance. I promise I won't screw up. I work for a very rich man right now and I can afford Rosalinda's treatment."

"We don't need your money. We're doing perfectly fine without you."

He looked so crestfallen that I wanted to hug him, but I would never hug a stranger, and to me he was just that.

I didn't give him a chance to say anything else as I turned around and opened the door then closed it behind me. I peeked out of the window beside the front door and saw him still standing where I had left him.

I couldn't see what he did next because my phone started ringing. I ran to my bedroom and picked it up without checking who was calling me.

"Hello?"

"Why aren't you answering your phone?" Collin asked in a worried voice.

"I was at the grocery store and I forgot my phone at home." I told him as I sat down on the bed.

"Do you know how worried I was? I was going to come over to check that everything was fine. Don't you ever do that again!" He scolded me like I was a five year old.

"I'm sorry that you got worried, and I'm sorry that I forgot my phone. I will wear it around my neck next time. Any more orders, sir?" I spat out; my tone was cold and angry. Before Collin could say anything, I hung up on him and screamed in frustration.

What was my dad doing here? What did he want from us now? He had left us, left his sick daughter, his wife who loved him so much. He left me, his daughter, who loved him, who looked up at him as her hero, as a role model. He walked away when we needed him most.

I willed my thoughts to go away as I stood up and walked out of my room and in to the kitchen, and started to make the lasagna and onion soup.

About half an hour later, I heard a knock on the door. I peeked out of the window and saw Collin standing there with an angry look on his face.

I gulped and opened the door. Collin looked at me through narrowed eyes. I didn't say anything, and just stood aside to let him in.

"Care to explain?" Collin asked as he stood in the middle of the living room with a displeased look on his face.

"I'm sorry?" It sounded more of a question than a statement. I knew that what I did was wrong. I shouldn't have yelled at him.

"You're asking me?" He looked at me incredulously. "I don't appreciate being yelled at, Esmeralda."

"I'm sorry, I really am." I said as I sat down on the couch. "I've had a crappy day and I guess you were on the receiving end of that."

Collin sighed and sat down beside me. "What's wrong, baby? What happened?"

"It's just been one of those days, you know?" I wasn't going to tell him about my dad. He didn't need to know.

Collin didn't push any further and just hugged me tightly against his body. I wrapped my arms around him and relished in his touch. That was exactly what I needed.

He pulled back and looked at me. "I'll let it go this time. However, if you yell at me one more time then there will consequences." He warned.

"What are you going to do? Spank me?" I asked sarcastically and chuckled.

"Maybe I might." He said seriously.

"You wouldn't dare." I said as I stood up.

"Try me." He challenged with a smirk.

#

"Did anything interesting happen at school today?" I asked Rosalinda as we sat at the table eating lunch.

Collin left shortly after our conversation saying that he had an important meeting to attend to.

"Same old, same old" She said with a shrug.

"What about you, honey?" My mom asked me this time. "Anything interesting?"

"No, no, nothing" I said as I stuffed my mouth with a big piece of lasagna. I wasn't going to tell my mom about my father coming to see us because I was sure that if she knew then she would forgive him instantly. Mom had a kind heart and she forgave quickly, but it wasn't the only reason that she would forgive him. Even though my mom never talked about him, I knew that she still loved him very much.

Suddenly, my sister's cell phone rang, but she didn't answer. "Aren't you going to answer?" I asked her.

"No."

I looked at my mom then back at her. "Why? Who is calling you?"

"It's just a friend from school. They want to go to the mall, but I told them I don't want to. I don't know why they're still calling." She said with a shrug as she pushed her food around her plate.

"Why don't you want to go?" My mom asked her.

Rosalinda just shrugged. "They're rich kids. They'll probably buy a lot of things while I'll just look with my eyes." She said, looking down at her plate.

"Call them back and tell them you're going." I told her sternly.

"But..." She started to complain when I stopped her.

"I'll give you money so you can buy whatever you want as well."

A bright smile made its way to Rosalinda's face. She picked up her phone and stood up from the table to call her friends while mom and I grabbed the empty plates to the kitchen.

A little while later, Rosalinda appeared at the kitchen door and informed us that her friends would be picking her up to go to the mall.

"If you need anything, Rosa, just ask me or mom."

"Yes, sweetie" Mom agreed. "You know that you can ask us for anything."

"I know." She said in a low voice. "It's just that both of you have been working really hard and I don't want to take your money."

I looked at my sister disbelievingly. "Don't you ever think that way, Rosa. You are a part of our family." I gave my sister a wide smile and hugged her then mom joined in on the hug.

#

Joe walked me out of the strip club and hailed a taxi for me. I thanked him and stepped inside the taxi.

I was tired and just wanted to go to sleep. It wasn't long until the taxi stopped in front of my house. I paid the driver and stepped out of the car then started walking towards my door when my cell phone rang. I looked at the screen and Collin's name appeared.

"Hello?" I answered.

"Turn around."

I did as told and saw his car parked at the other side of the road. I had a smile on my face as I walked towards him and hung up midway. I opened the passenger's seat door and stepped inside.

"Hey, handsome" I placed a kiss on his cheek. "Why are you here?"

"I wanted to see my beautiful girlfriend." He said seriously. "I missed you."

"Well, I missed you too." I leaned forward and placed a soft kiss on his lips.

Collin, however, seemed to have other ideas as he pulled me up and awkwardly placed me on his lap. I giggled and sat up straight then wrapped my arms around his neck. I parted my lips for him and he wasted no time as he slipped in his tongue in a sweet invasion. Our tongues fought for dominance as I fed from the sweetness of his mouth. Collin kissed me with hungry urgency and he started roaming his hands on my upper body before it came to rest on my butt; pulling me closer to him. I moved back and forth; the friction from his jeans doing amazing things to my body. He moaned and pulled his head back, and I could feel him growing hard. He placed his hand on my waist; stopping me.

"Don't do that." His voice was strained.

"Why?" I whined as I started rocking my pelvis once more, but yet again he stopped me.

"I won't be able to stop myself and I would take you right here, right now." He said seriously and that made me stop what I was doing.

I captured his lips in one last long, drugging kiss before I pulled back and pulled up from him then sat back down at the passenger's seat. I rested my head back and closed my eyes.

"I wish I could stay here with you forever."

"We can't stay here forever." Collin said and I opened my eyes and looked sideways at him. "But you do have me forever." He said more softly as he leaned forward and pressed a soft, lingering kiss on my lips.

"I love you." He said in a whisper as he pulled back. I looked at him wide eyed. Did I hear that right? "You don't have to say it back or anything. It just came out. I'm sorry."

"I love you too." I said honestly. Collin had been nothing but good to me. Even when he knew I was a stripper, he treated me no different than he would treat any other woman.

A smile made its way to Collin's face. "You have no idea how happy this makes me." He held my face in his hands and kissed me slowly and sensually.

"I have to go inside." I said as I pulled back.

He looked at me lovingly. "Goodnight, beautiful."

"Goodnight, handsome." I placed one last kiss on his lips before stepping out of the car.

**********Remember to vote, comment, share, recommend, add 'Trixie' to your reading list, and follow. :)

Chapter 13 - The Big Fight and Moving Out

"One chocolate chip cookie dough with brownie chunks and one peanut butter fudge with caramel sauce on top." The young man said with a smile as he handed Rosalinda and I our ice creams. "Would you like anything else?" He asked us politely.

"No, thank you. That will be it."

The young man nodded then pressed some buttons on the register. "That will be eleven dollars."

I handed him the money then Rosalinda and I went to sit at a small table.

"Is it good?" I asked my sister and she nodded with a grin.

"Better than I remember."

I nodded with a smile and licked my ice cream. I rarely ate fatty foods since I didn't want to gain weight and lose my job, but I figured it wouldn't hurt if I had one with my sister. She had said during lunch how much she was craving an ice cream, and I was happy that she was starting to get her appetite back.

"How is Collin?" She asked me.

"He's good." I replied as I licked my ice cream. "I haven't talked to him today yet."

"Why?" She asked me.

"He's probably busy at work." I shrugged as I licked some more.

"I like him." She told me. "I think he's good for you. You deserve someone like him."

I looked up at my sister with a sincere smile on my face. "He is good, isn't he?" I asked myself more than her. "I told him I love him."

"What did he say?" She asked excitedly; her ice cream all forgotten about.

I chuckled. "Well, he said it first."

"No way!" She said with a happy smile. "I'm so happy for you, Es. I hope I'll get to see your wedding day."

I looked at my sister with a determined look on my face. "First of all, it's too early to be thinking or talking about weddings. Second of all, you will be able to see my wedding day, if I get married. Nothing will happen to you. You are a strong girl. Do you understand?"

"Yes." She gave me a wide smile then continued licking her ice cream.

We sat there for a little while longer before we headed back home. There was a fancy car parked in our driveway. I parked mom's old blue beetle that I had borrowed beside the fancy car and stepped out.

"Who do you think is here?" I asked Rosalinda with a confused look on my face. We rarely had visitors over.

"Maybe it's Collin?" She asked with a shrug.

"No, this is not his car." I told her.

Neither of us said anything else. We walked up to the front door and I brought out my keys and opened it. Rosalinda went in first and I followed, closing the door behind me. We heard chattering and laughter, and I got even more intrigued about knowing who was making my mother laugh that much. However, when I walked in to the living room, I froze in my spot. I closed my eyes and opened them; trying to get myself to wake up from this nightmare, but nope he was still there; looking at me with a hopeful smile.

"Dad?" Rosalinda asked softly; the happiness she was feeling was heard clearly in her tone. She walked towards him and he stood up, pulling her into a hug.

"What are you doing here?" My tone was harsh and cold.

"Your father is moving back in, and he's willing to pay for Rosalinda's treatment." My mother explained happily.

I looked at my dad with narrowed eyes. "I specifically told you that we didn't need your money. We are doing perfectly fine without you. You can go back to where you came from."

"Esmeralda!" My mom scolded.

I turned to look at my mom. "What, mom? Did he tell you that he was working for a rich man? Did he tell you how he was going to stick around this time? Did he put in some sweet words to make you take him back?" I yelled.

"How... how did you know?" My mom asked me.

"He visited a couple of days ago. He wanted to see his family." I scoffed.

"Why didn't you tell me?" She asked in a low voice.

"Why? So you could take him back? So he could hurt us again?" My mom looked at the ground. I turned to look at my father. "We don't want you here. Leave us alone!"

"You're my family. How can I leave you alone?"

"Funny how you didn't have a problem with leaving us the first time around."

My father ran his hand through his hair and sighed. "Es, I couldn't handle everything that was happening. I wasn't able to afford the treatment. You have to understand."

I looked at the person I called my father disbelievingly. "So you just leave your daughter like she's some stranger that you picked up from the street? Mom and I weren't able to afford the treatment either, but we worked hard so we could be able to pay for Rosa's treatment. Did you once think to ask about her? Huh?" I yelled angrily.

"Enough, Esmeralda! This is your father."

I scoffed and looked at my mom. "I cannot believe you. After everything he put us through, you still defend him."

"He is your father, and you will respect him!" She said; ignoring my accusation. "He is moving in and that's it!"

"No, no, no way!" I laughed humorlessly.

"Es, please..." My father started, but I stopped him.

"Do not talk to me!" I pointed a finger at him then turned towards my mom.

"If he moves in, I move out!" Everyone was quiet, even my mom. You could hear a pin drop in the room. I couldn't believe what was happening.

I turned my back, walked to my room, and closed the door behind me. I grabbed my duffel bag from my closet and grabbed whatever clothes came in my way and threw them in. I was not going to stay one second at home with him here. I suddenly heard someone knock on the door, but I didn't answer. A second later, the door opened slightly and Rosalinda slipped in. She walked slowly towards me and looked at me with sad eyes.

"You're really leaving the house?"

"Yes." I said; my features softening as I saw how sad she looked.

"Please, don't go." She pleaded as she walked towards me.

"I'm sorry, Rosa, but I can't stay in the same house as him."

"Then I want to leave with you."

I sighed and sat down on the bed. Rosalinda came and sat down beside me. I turned sideways and looked at her. "Rosa, sweetie, I know you don't want to do that. I saw how happy you were when you saw him, and you have every right to be; he is your dad after all."

"Then why are you leaving?"

"I can't forgive him for what he has done. I don't want you to hate him, Rosa. He's our dad. Maybe one day I'll find it in my heart to forgive him, just like you and mom did, but for now I just can't."

"Will you come visit us at least?" She asked me with hopeful eyes.

I shook my head. "Not anytime soon, sweetie, but you can come visit me anytime."

"Where are you going to stay?" She asked me with a worried tone.

"I'm not sure yet. I'll probably stay at some cheap hotel until I could figure things out."

Rosalinda didn't say anything. Instead, she leaned forward and pulled me into a hug. She hugged me so tight as if afraid that I would disappear at any moment. Pulling back from the hug, I looked at her and watched as a tear slid down her face.

"Don't cry, Rosa." I soothed. "You will see me and talk to me every day. I promise."

"Pinky promise?" She asked me as she held out her pinky finger.

I chuckled and hooked my pinky around her little finger. "Pinky promise"

We both stood up and I continued throwing things into my duffel bag. When I had packed everything, I zipped up my bag and placed it around my shoulder. I looked around my room; checking if I had missed something before I opened the door and walked out with Rosalinda behind me. We walked into the living room where my mom and father were sitting silently. They both looked up at me, and I was sure that they both noticed the duffel bag on my shoulder, but they didn't say anything and neither did I. I walked to the front door, and heard Rosalinda's soft footsteps behind me. As we reached the front door, I turned around and hugged my sister.

"If you need anything, Rosa, call me. Okay?" I told her as I pulled back. She nodded sadly and waved goodbye.

I hailed a taxi and stepped inside. I didn't know where to tell him to take me because I didn't know where to go. Eventually, I told him to take me to the nearest motel. Once we arrived at our destination, I stepped out of the car. I felt shivers run down my spine as I looked at the old motel. I looked back as the taxi drove away before walking towards the reception desk which was empty. There was, however, a small bell atop of the desk so I rang it. An old man appeared and looked at me with a bored expression on his face.

"How can I help you?" He asked.

"Do you have an empty room?"

#

I placed my bag on the ground and sat down on the creaking bed then looked around the small room that had chipped walls. It looked like it needed to be repainted. There was also a weird smell coming from the bathroom, but I shrugged knowing I had no other choice. I brought my phone out of my pocket and dialed Collin's number, he answered on the third ring.

"Hey, beautiful"

"Hey, are you busy?" I asked him.

"A little bit. Is everything okay?" he sounded worried.

"Yes, um..." I rubbed my forehead. "Can you come to Sunrise Rainbow Motel? It's a couple of streets down from my house." To my disappointment and confusion, I didn't get a response. Instead, I heard the dial tone. I removed the cell phone from my ear and looked at it for a moment before I fell back on the bed and let the tears fall freely down my face.

**********Remember to vote, comment, share, recommend, add 'Trixie' to your reading list, and follow. :)

Chapter 14 - Moving In

A knock on the door startled me awake.

I didn't notice myself falling asleep. I guess it must have been all the crying that made my body lose all the energy and fall asleep. I stood up from the bed and walked over to the door. I was about to ask who it was until another knock was heard.

"Open up, Es!" I quickly realized that this was Collin's voice, and he was angry.

I opened the door and he didn't say anything. He just pushed me aside and walked in. I closed the door behind him then stood with my back against it and watched him as he stood in the middle of the room with an angry look on his face.

"Why are you here?"

"I moved out." I said as I moved away from the door and walked closer to him.

"Why?" He asked; his whole expression changing to that of a confused one.

"Mom and I had a fight so..." I sat down on the bed. "I left."

He walked towards me and sat down beside me on the bed. "Do you want to talk about it?" He asked me softly.

I shook my head. "Not right now."

Collin nodded understandingly then stood up and looked around the room. "Where are your bags?"

I pointed to where it was beside the door. "I only have one bag."

He walked towards it and picked it up. "Come on, let's go."

I looked at him with a confused look on my face. "Go where? I have nowhere else to go."

"We're going to my house." He replied simply. "Did you really think I would let you stay in this dodgy place?"

"It is not dodgy." I lied. "It's... okay." I seemed to be at loss for a better word.

"Do you have anything else you want to take?" He asked me; ignoring what had said.

"Collin." I stood up. "I'm not going anywhere."

Collin didn't respond to me. Instead, he walked to the bathroom then came out a second later. He then looked around the room as if trying to search for something before grabbing my hand, opening the door and walking out.

He took us to the reception desk and rang the bell. The same old man appeared and looked at Collin before transferring his gaze to me.

"Going with the boyfriend I see?" He asked.

"Where is the key, Es?" Collin asked me as he looked sideways at me; ignoring the old man's comment. I reluctantly brought it out of my jeans pocket and gave it to him. Collin took it from me and handed it to the old man. "I would like a refund as well."

"What refund are you talking about, young man? Ten minutes had already passed." The man could sense that Collin was ready to argue so he quickly said. "I can refund you for the next day she paid for." He said as he handed Collin the forty six dollars I had paid.

Collin glared at the old man before taking the money from him. "Let's go." He said as we walked towards his car.

He handed my bag to his driver who placed it in the trunk before opening the car door for us. Once we were settled inside, Collin ordered his driver to take us to his penthouse then handed me my money.

"Thank you." I gave him a small smile as I accepted the money from him and placed it in my pocket. He placed his arm around my shoulder and pulled me to him as I rested my head on his chest.

It wasn't long before the car stopped in front of a very luxurious looking building. The driver opened Collin's door before opening mine. I thanked him and stepped out of the car. Collin snaked his arm around my waist and ordered his driver to take my bag to the penthouse.

"It's fine. I can take it."

"No." Collin replied; not giving me a chance to argue as he started walking inside the building.

The concierge greeted him as we passed by and then walked towards one of the elevators. His driver was right behind us. The elevator dinged, signaling its arrival and we all entered. Collin pressed the top floor button then added a code, and soft music started playing in the background. With Collin's arm still around my waist, he pulled me closer to him. I looked up at him and gave him a small smile. Once again, the elevator dinged and the doors opened to a lavish looking penthouse.

"Do you need anything else, sir?" I heard the driver asking Collin, but I was too busy looking at the penthouse to even listen to what Collin said to him in reply.

"Do you like it?" Collin asked me as I felt his arm on my waist.

I looked up at him with a smile. "Yes, it's perfect."

He walked me to the living room which looked very modern yet cozy at the same time, and sat down on one of the couches.

"Would you like to drink something?" He asked me.

I looked up at him. "A cup of water, please." He nodded and walked away. I took the chance to look around the living room.

There was a small bar behind me, and the living room overlooked green scenery which was breathtaking. The color theme was mainly white which gave it that cozy feeling, incorporated with a little bit of grey and metallic.

"Here you go." Collin said as he handed me the cup of water and sat down beside me. I thanked him and took a small sip to quench my thirst then placed the cup on the glass coffee table.

"Do you want to talk now?"

I turned sideways and looked at him.

"My father is moving back in and my mom took him in with open arms and basically threw her daughter out." I told him the short version. Collin looked at me with a confused expression on his face so I decided to elaborate. "I was out with Rosa, and when we came back home we found my father sitting in the living room with my mom like nothing had happened before. Mom then tells me that he's moving back in. I lost it and started a fight with her then told her that if he moves in, I move out. She didn't talk me out of it so I just packed a bag and left. She didn't try to stop me on my way out which is what hurt most. She chose my father over me; the father that abandoned us." I didn't know I was crying until Collin placed his thumb under my eyes and wiped away my tears.

"Your mom loves you, baby."

"Yeah, it shows." I laughed humorlessly. Collin didn't say anything and just hugged me to his chest. He moved his hand up and down my back in a soothing manner. I grabbed fistfuls of his shirt and just hugged him tighter.

"I love you." My voice was muffled against his chest.

Collin pulled back from the hug and looked straight into my eyes. "I love you too, beautiful." He leaned forward and kissed my forehead.

I noticed that the sun was setting down. "Are you hungry?" I asked him.

"Yes, do you want us to order something?"

"I was wondering if I could cook instead." I said shyly.

"You're tired, baby. Let's just order something."

"Cooking gets my mind off things." I told him.

"Okay." He accepted then stood up and outstretched his hand for me to take. "Come on; let me show you the kitchen." I placed my hand in his and stood up as I let him lead me to the kitchen. We walked in to a stunning open-plan kitchen. "The fridge and cupboards are fully stocked with everything you might need."

I looked at him sideways. "Do you stock them?"

He shook his head no. "I have a cook to do that for me."

"You have a cook?" I asked disbelievingly.

Collin chuckled. "Yes, I don't have time to cook." He came towards me and kissed the side of my head.

I gave him a smile then opened the fridge and looked inside trying to figure out what to cook. "What would you like to eat?" I asked him; not looking at him.

"Whatever you want, beautiful." He hugged me from behind. I turned my head sideways and he placed a kiss on my lips then released his hand. "I'm going to take your stuff to the room." He informed me and I nodded thankfully.

About an hour later, Collin appeared in the kitchen with a smile on his face. "What is this heavenly aroma?" He asked.

"Chicken in creamy mushroom sauce and spicy baked potato wedges" I informed him.

"Sounds delicious, do you want any help?"

I gave him a thankful smile and shook my head. "I'm already done, babe."

We sat at the round table in the kitchen and ate the dinner I had prepared. Collin praised my cooking skills saying that I even cooked better than his mom, but made me promise not to tell her. When we finished eating, I placed the empty dishes in the dishwasher then dried them off and placed them back to their places.

Collin and I retired to the living room and watched TV. I curled up on the couch and rested my head on his chest as he brought a blanket from beside him and covered me up. He placed his arm around my shoulder and brought me closer to him.

"Can I be brutally honest, baby?" He asked me and I hesitantly nodded. "I'm glad that you had a fight with your mom because now you're here." He gave me a guilty smile.

"Am I a bad daughter if I say I'm glad as well?"

Collin sighed in relief. "No, not at all, baby." He kissed the side of my head.

A couple of hours later, I started yawning. This went unnoticed by Collin as he asked. "Do you want to go to sleep?"

"No, no." I waved him off.

"Okay." He said amused. A couple of minutes later, I started yawning again and my eyes starting closing shut.

Collin stood up. "Come on, beautiful, let's go to bed." This time I didn't argue and let him lead me to his room.

We walked in to his room. It looked nice, just like the rest of the penthouse, but I was too sleepy to really pay attention to details. He walked me in to his en suite bathroom that was huge with a fancy looking Jacuzzi in the middle. I could definitely make use of that.

"There's an extra toothbrush in the medicine cabinet." He told me. "If you need anything else I'll be in the room."

I nodded gratefully and watched him as he walked out and closed the door behind him.

I walked out of the bathroom and saw Collin lying on the bed with no t-shirt on. I moved my gaze away and walked to my suitcase that was atop one of the chairs. I unzipped the bag and rummaged through my clothes trying to find something to sleep in. Eventually, I found a baby doll that I must have threw in when I was packing. I grabbed it, zipped up my bag, and walked back in to the bathroom. I changed into my baby doll and placed my dirty clothes in the hamper then walked back out.

Collin's eyes widened as he saw me walk towards the bed. I crawled under the covers and scooted closer to him.

"Do you always sleep like this?" He asked me and I nodded. "You're killing me." He closed his eyes for a moment and I chuckled. I rested my head on his chest and he started smoothing down my hair. "Baby, I think you should forgive your dad."

I pulled back and looked at him. "If you don't want me here, I can find somewhere else to stay."

"No, no." Collin said as he sat up straight. "I couldn't be any happier that you're here." The sincerity could be heard clearly in his voice. "What I mean is he's your dad. You can't hold a grudge forever."

I rested my head back on his chest. "I can't find it in me to forgive him now. I really don't. Maybe in the future I will, but not now."

"Okay." Collin kissed the side of my head, and didn't push any further.I looked up at him and placed a soft kiss on his lips before closing my eyes and falling into deep sleep.

**********Remember to vote, comment, share, recommend, add 'Trixie' to your reading list, and follow. :)

Chapter 15 - Shopping Spree

I woke up the next morning feeling more refreshed than I had ever felt in a long time.

I looked up at Collin who looked like an angel as he slept. I studied his features for a moment, and couldn't help but wonder how I got this lucky. I looked at the clock that was on his night stand and noticed that it was seven a.m. I placed a soft kiss on his chest and softly removed the duvet from my body and stood up from the bed as carefully as I could so that I wouldn't wake Collin up then walked in to the bathroom.

I looked at Collin as I walked out of the bathroom and noticed that he was still fast asleep. I wanted to do something special for him so I tiptoed out of the room and walked to the kitchen. I remembered Collin said that his fridge was fully stocked, so I brought out all the necessary ingredients out and started preparing breakfast.

About an hour later, I was holding a tray that held a plate of Chocolate chip heart shaped pancakes, French toast with honey and berries, bacon, omelet, and two cups of tea. I walked back to the room where I saw Collin still asleep. I placed the tray on the table beside the couch then crawled back into bed.

Afraid that the breakfast would go cold, I decided to wake Collin up. I started trailing feather-like kisses along his chest down to his abdomen, and he groaned. I took that as a good sign and continued to trail those feather-like kisses, but this time upwards. As soon as I reached his chest I saw his eyes open.

"What a wonderful way to wake up." His voice was hoarse.

I grinned and placed a chaste kiss on his lips. "Good morning, my love. I made you breakfast."

He brought his arm down to my waist and pulled me close against him.

"Just stay here for a moment."

I wrapped my arm around his waist and rested my head on his chest.

"What time did you wake up, beautiful?" His chest vibrated with every word he said.

"About an hour ago"

"Why didn't you wake me up?"

"You looked so innocent while you were sleeping. I didn't have the heart to wake you up." I looked up at him through my lashes and he had a smile on his face.

"I love you. Do you know that?"

"I love you too." I raised myself up a bit and placed a soft kiss on those tasty lips of his. "Breakfast's getting cold. Come on." I stood up from the bed and Collin followed then we sat down around the small round table.

"Did you cook all of this?" Collin asked me amazed and I nodded with a grin.

"You're spoiling me, baby. I could get used to this."

"I want you to get used to this because you won't be getting anything less." He leaned over the table and pecked my lips.

We ate the breakfast I prepared and once again Collin rained me with praises. Once we finished, Collin went to his office to work a bit while I took a shower. As I walked out after my shower with nothing but a towel covering my naked body, I saw Collin sitting on the bed with a smirk on his face and looking fresh and clean.

"Did you take a shower?" I asked him and he nodded.

"I took a shower in the other room after I finished my calls."

I nodded then walked to my suitcase and unzipped it. I grabbed the first pair of panties and bra that I saw then grabbed a pair of jeans and a top.

"Baby, when are you going to put your clothes in the closet?" Collin asked me.

I turned around and looked at him as I held my clothes in my hand. "I don't know." I said dejectedly. "If I do, it would feel like this is it, it's real, I moved out. Does it make sense?"

"It does, baby. You have to accept it though." He stood up from the bed and walked towards me. "Even when you do make up with your mom, I'm not letting you move out of here so you might as well get used to the idea." I smiled at the possessiveness of the man in front of me; my man.

I placed a soft and chaste kiss on his lips then walked back to the bathroom with Collin's eyes following my every move. I knew that I could have just changed in the room since he had already seen me naked. Well, without a bra at least, but for some reason I felt uncomfortable changing in front of him.

I walked out of the bathroom after I had changed into my jeans and top, and found Collin sitting on the bed. He tapped his lap and I eagerly walked over to him and sat down. He wrapped his arm around my waist while I wrapped my arms around his neck.

"What do you want to do today, beautiful?" He asked me. "It's a Sunday so you have me all to yourself."

I shrugged. "I don't care, as long as I'm with you." I gave him a wide smile.

"I have something in mind."

"What is it?" I asked him intrigued with what he might have planned for us.

"What do you think about shopping?"

"No shops are open on a Sunday, babe." I chuckled.

"You'd be amazed what money could do." He said.

A little while later we were in his car as he drove us to our destination. It wasn't long until we arrived at a shop that looked too pricey from the outside for me to ever go inside. Collin parked the car and a man opened my door. I thanked him and watched as Collin came to my side and placed his arm around my waist as we made our way inside the store.

"Mr. Edwards, how are you?" A bald man quickly walked towards Collin and shook his hand.

"I'm fine, Mr. Wilson." He answered formally. "This is the woman I was telling you about." Collin said and the bald man, Mr. Wilson, moved his gaze towards me before looking back at Collin. "I want you to give her whatever she asks for, regardless of the price."

Mr. Wilson nodded eagerly then turned sideways. "Lauren, please come and help this lovely lady with whatever she needs." Lauren nodded and walked towards me and started leading me towards the dresses.

"Can I offer you some champagne while you wait, Mr. Edwards?" I heard Mr. Wilson ask as I walked away.

About an hour later I had tried out several rompers, tops, trousers, skirts, dresses, just about everything, but I didn't settle on anything though because each one of them cost more than a night's work at the strip club.

"Hey, Lauren?" I walked out of the dressing room.

"Yes, is something wrong?" She asked me worriedly.

"No, everything's fine." I gave her a grateful smile.

"Do you not like the clothes?" She asked me, probably noticing that I had come out empty handed.

"Yes, I do, but I need to talk to Collin."

She nodded and walked me to him. He was sitting at one of the couches in the lounge area, sipping on his champagne and concentrating on something on his phone. He probably heard my footsteps because he looked up at me.

"Did you not like anything?" He asked me.

"I did." I said as I walked over to him and sat down beside him. "They're really pricey, Collin." I whispered so no one would hear me. "I already have a lot of clothes. I don't need anymore."

Collin didn't reply. Instead, he looked at Lauren. "We'll take everything she tried on."

"Collin!" I whisper yelled.

"Also," He continued ignoring me. "I want you give her some evening dresses to try on." He ordered. Lauren nodded with a smile and waited for me to stand up.

"Collin, I really don't need those."

Collin this time didn't ignore me and looked at me. "I have the money, beautiful, and it is my pleasure to be spending it on you." A small smile made its way to my face even though I didn't like him spending money on me.

I stood up and walked over to Lauren who handed me several evening gowns to try on. After several gowns later, I had still not liked a single one. Lauren then handed me a dress from behind the door.

"Mr. Edwards wants you to try this on." She told me as she handed me the dress. "He also wants to see you in it."

I accepted the dress from her and closed the door. I hung the dress on the hook that was on the door and looked at it. It was a burgundy colored floor-length dress that appeared to have a sweep train. I tried the dress on and looked at the floor length mirror in the dressing room. The dress looked stunning on me. Suddenly, I heard a knock on the door.

"Mrs. Roberts." I heard Lauren's voice. "Mr. Edwards would like to see you."

I unlocked the door and walked out to where Collin was sitting with Lauren on my heels. Collin looked at me with his mouth wide open. It took him a moment to recover before he said.

"We'll take this." I smiled and walked over to him. "You look stunning." He commented. The sincerity in his words could be clearly heard. I gave him a peck on the lips then went back to the dressing room to change.

#

"Thank you, Cole." Collin thanked the concierge and tipped him before he left.

I walked over to Collin, stood on my tippy toes, and pressed a hot scorching kiss on his lips. "Thank you, handsome."

"You deserve more, beautiful." He said in a husky voice.

#

Later that night, I stood in front of my mirror, dressed up in the floor length dress Collin had brought me.

Collin had asked me to wear it, saying he wanted to take me somewhere special. I had already done my makeup and was ready to go when I saw Collin, from my vanity mirror, opening the door and entering.

"You look utterly beautiful." He walked towards me and hugged me from behind. I turned around in his embrace and hugged him back. "Turn around." He ordered. I looked up at him questioningly, but did as told.

I watched as he brought a box out of his pocket, opened it, and revealed a beautiful diamond necklace. He placed it around my neck and I placed my hand on it.

"This is beautiful, when did you get it?"

"When you were in the dressing room"

I turned around and looked at Collin lovingly. "I love you."

"I love you too, beautiful."

A little while later, Collin drove us to our destination. He wouldn't tell me where though. About half an hour later, the car came to a stop in front of a fancy hotel, and a man opened Collin's door while another one opened mine. I stepped out of the car, thanked the man, and watched as Collin handed him his car keys before he came around to my side, snaked his arm around my waist and walked us inside.

**********Remember to vote, comment, share, recommend, add 'Trixie' to your reading list, and follow. :)

Chapter 16 - Night of Passion

Collin walked us to one of the restaurants that were located on the ground floor.

As soon as we walked inside, the head-waiter greeted Collin and led us to a small round table in the middle that had one red candle in the center.

Collin pushed back my chair for me to sit down before he sat down in his chair that was opposite of mine. I looked around the restaurant and noticed that it was empty.

"Babe" I whispered, gaining Collin's attention. "Why is the restaurant empty?"

Collin smirked before saying. "It's ours for the night."

I gasped and looked at him wide eyed. He had rented the restaurant. Why do we need the whole restaurant to ourselves? I thought to myself, but before I could dwell on that thought, the waiter approached our table with a tray that held two bowls of soup. He placed one of the bowls in front of me then placed the other one in front of Collin before walking away.

"I hope its fine that I had already ordered."

I smiled at Collin. "It's fine. I don't mind."

Collin gave me a smile before we both started digging in. It was creamy mushroom soup, and it tasted great. I left a little bit in the bowl because I didn't want to get full when I hadn't even eaten the main course.

Once we were both done, Collin gestured for the waiter to come. He picked up the empty bowls then came back with a tray that held two very yummy looking creamy steaks. He placed the plates in front of Collin and I then left. They looked too good that I didn't waste any time before I started digging in.

"You're done?" Collin asked me as I pushed the half empty plate away.I nodded. "I'm full. I can't eat anymore."

"There's still dessert." He said.

"Well, I was thinking about a different kind of dessert." I purred as I leaned forward.

Collin's eyes darkened. "Don't tease me, Es."

I had a teasing smile on my face as I sat back straight. "I want you, Collin." My breathy tone was more of a whisper.

No other words were needed as Collin stood up from his seat and walked to my side. He held my hand and started to walk out.

"Aren't you going to pay?" I asked him.

"Everything's paid for." He said; not looking at me as he kept walking towards the reception desk. It was like he was a man on a mission.

#

"What do you mean there are no available rooms?" Collin argued.

"I'm sorry, sir, but we are fully booked. The only suite we have available is the presidential suite."

"We'll take it." Collin said without missing a heartbeat.

"Collin" I whisper yelled, but he ignored me.

He took the card key from the young man at the reception then held my hand as we walked to the elevators. As soon as the elevator doors closed, I turned to Collin and looked up at him.

"Collin, this is too much."

Instead of replying, I felt myself being softly pushed against the elevator wall and Collin's lips captured mine in a raw, deep, and passionate kiss. I wrapped my arms around his neck and brought him closer to me as I opened my mouth and he quickly slipped his tongue inside. His tongue roamed inside my mouth as if searching for something and his hands slid down the sides of my body.

Just then, the elevator dinged announcing its arrival to our floor. Collin and I broke up the kiss as we both breathed heavily. He held my hand and we started walking out while I tried to catch my breath.

Collin opened the door and I entered before him and looked around the huge room. I heard the door closing shut then gasped as Collin, in a sudden move, held me bridal style and started walking towards the bedroom. He placed me gently on the king size bed and just stood there. I crawled on all fours towards him and was about to undo his pants when he held my hand stopping me. I looked up at him questioningly.

"Stand up." He ordered. I did as told and he sat down on the bed. "I want to see you undress."

I looked at him through my eyelashes. "I want you to undress me."

His gaze roamed my body before he stood up and stood behind me. He started raining kisses down my neck and I leaned my neck to the other side to give him more access. His hands moved up and down my body then one of his hand disappeared and I felt him unzipping my dress slowly, sensually, and teasingly before it pooled on the floor around my feet. I turned around and looked at Collin who was looking at me through dark eyes as I stood there in nothing but my lingerie. I started to unbutton his shirt all the while looking at him as he held my gaze. Once I threw his shirt on the floor, I started to work on his pants. I fumbled with his belt as I tried to unbuckle it then removed it and unbuttoned his pants. They fell to the floor just like my dress had earlier. Collin's hands went behind me as he removed my bra, in one swift move. He started walking closer to me while I walked backwards until my legs hit the bed. Collin pushed me back on the bed so that I was lying on my back as he crawled on top of me while he balanced his weight on his hands. We held each other's gazes for a moment before his mouth found my breast.

"Oh!" I moaned at the amazing sensation.

I slid my fingers through his hair, needing something to hold on to. He kissed the tight nub and a hot tension started building within me. His hand found my other breast, and he rolled the nipple between his thumb and forefinger in a slow motion. I arched my chest, wanting to give him everything. His mouth moved to the other breast that needed his attention as well. He sucked and bit on the nipple as he caressed the other one with his thumb. I was going to burst. I couldn't breathe anymore. He raised his head up and kissed my lips before moving down and hooking his hands in my pants. He looked up at me as if searching for approval and I gave him a reassuring smile. He slid down my pants and I heard him suck in a breath before his head disappeared between my legs.

"Oh, god" I moaned in pleasure as I arched my back and grabbed a fistful of Collin's hair. "Oh, Collin" I cried out his name as my whole body convulsed in a chain of spasms. Collin looked up at me with a smirk before he came all the way up and kissed my lips hungrily. He skilfully turned us over so that I was straddling him. I pulled back from the kiss breathless and hooked my hands in his briefs before pulling it down.

"I want to touch you." I told him and he nodded.

I reached for him, and my hands slipped around him, adoring him with my touch. I heard Collin hiss in pleasure as he leaned his head back. Feeling brave, I bent my head down and wrapped my lips around his length as I looked up at him through my lashes.

"Oh god, oh god" He moaned as he ran his hand through his hair, unknowingly letting me know that I was doing something right, and giving me the confidence to go on.

I bobbed my head up and down, and occasionally looked up at him. He cupped my face with his hands as I pulled back for air then pulled me up to him. He kissed me passionately before turning us around so that he was back on top of me. He dipped his head and kissed my lips. He slipped his velvety tongue in and out of my mouth as his hand rested on one of my breasts.

Suddenly, I felt him pushing my thighs apart.

"Wider, baby" He said as his hand rubbed down my center. "You're wet for me." He smirked, and I nodded embarrassedly as my cheeks flushed.

He dipped his head and captured my lips with his, and suddenly, I felt him plunge one finger inside then he started to rub my sensitive spot making me see stars. I pulled back from the kiss and arched my back as I moaned in ecstasy. It wasn't long before my whole body convulsed in a chain of spasms. Collin removed his hand and licked it whilst looking me in the eye. He then kissed me as I tasted my juices in his mouth.

He started positioning himself between my legs and he looked straight into my eyes as if asking if I wanted to go on. It was too late to go back now that I've tasted a piece of heaven.

Without a warning, Collin plunged himself inside of me and I squeezed my eyes shut in slight pain as a tear slid down my eye. Once I opened them, I saw Collin frozen in place with a shocked and fearful expression on his face.

"Why did you stop?" I asked him confused.

"You're a virgin." He stated, and I nodded. "Why didn't you tell me?" He asked in a low voice.

"I don't know. I was ashamed." My voice was low.

Collin sighed and my heart started beating. He regrets this. He doesn't want me anymore. I thought to myself, afraid that he would leave me.

"You should have told me, Es. I wouldn't have rushed into this. You deserve more than this. Your first time should be special."

I looked at him as a smile made its way to my face. "It doesn't get more special than my first time being with you." I told him honestly and a small smile appeared on his face. "Now, please go on. You're killing me here." I whined.

Collin chuckled before he started moving again. "Tell me if it hurts, baby."

I nodded as I cupped his face with both of my hands and kissed him hungrily and passionately. The pain was slowly turning in pleasure and I arched my back as I moaned in ecstasy.

"Don't stop, harder." I moaned, and Collin complied.

I matched him thrust to thrust as our breathing became heavy. All of a sudden, everything started to tighten and my breathing got more difficult. I was close. I could feel it. I grabbed onto Collin's arm and squeezed as I started feeling light-headed and my vision was becoming blurry. My upper thighs started quivering and I broke into a light sweat. At that moment, I felt like everything disappeared except for that hot, tingly sensation that made me feel like I'm being pulled from all sides.

"Cum for me, baby."

It was all it took for me to lose myself. My whole body stopped moving, and I clenched up and enjoyed the explosion that erupted through my body. Collin groaned before I felt the hot spurt of him as he came inside me; filling me up.

He collapsed on the bed and pulled my head to rest on his chest as we both tried to regain our breaths.

"Are you okay?" Collin asked me as he smoothed my hair.

I looked up at him through my lashes. "Never been better" I assured him.

"You scared me, you know. It was like I lost you there for a second."

I turned over so that I was lying on my stomach. "It was like an out of body experience. It was so intense; I felt like my muscles just stopped working. It was like a volcanic eruption...but down there."

"I love you, Esmeralda." Collin leaned forwards and placed a soft kiss on my lips.

"I love you too." I said softly.

"Rest for a bit while I run you a hot bath, it will help you with the soreness." I nodded with a smile.

Collin stood up from the bed in all of his naked glory, and walked to the bathroom. I closed my eyes for a bit, feeling more relaxed that I had ever been in a long time.

"Bath is ready, baby." I heard Collin say.

I opened my eyes and saw him walking towards me. I stood up from the bed and met him halfway. He held be bridal style and walked me to the bathroom then placed me down gently in the bath tub. He settled himself behind me and wrapped his arms around me.

"Is the water okay?" He asked me.

"Yes, it's fine." I looked sideways at him with a small smile on my face.

Collin grabbed the soap from beside him and rubbed it all over my body so slowly and sensually. I felt so relaxed. Once we felt the water going cold, we stood up and Collin wrapped a towel around my body then dried himself off with another one before he held me once more and walked to the bedroom.

He placed me down on the bed, and my eyes slowly started to close shut before they snapped open and I looked at Collin.

"We didn't use a condom." I sat up straight and started to panic.

"Calm down, baby. We both got lost in the moment. Can't you take like a morning after pill or something?"

"Yes, but it doesn't work all the time."

"Let's take it one step at a time, baby. I'll get you the pills first thing tomorrow morning." I nodded. "Come on, let's sleep a bit." He brought me down to him and kissed my shoulder. "I love you." I heard him murmur.

I kissed his lips. "I love you too." I said honestly. Collin smoothed down my hair until I was fast asleep.

**********Remember to vote, comment, share, recommend, add 'Trixie' to your reading list, and follow. :)

Chapter 17 - Baby Talk

I woke up a couple of days later to painful cramps in my tummy.

I looked to the side and saw Collin sleeping like a baby. I removed the duvet from my body and stood up from the bed as quietly as I could so that I wouldn't wake Collin up. I walked to the bathroom and closed the door behind me, and sat down to pee then noticed there was blood in my pants. I changed quickly and washed my hands before I walked back out to the room.

I had a smile on my face as I crawled back to the bed and started poking Collin's shoulder to wake him up.

"Collin, wake up." He didn't wake up though.

I poked his shoulder once more, but still nothing so I removed the duvet and straddled him then started placing kisses on his chest. I heard him groan and my smile got even wider. I could feel his arousal growing, but I ignored it and looked up at him.

"Collin."

"Mm..." He answered his eyes still closed.

"I'm not pregnant." The happiness could be heard clearly in my voice.

Collin was wide awake as he looked at me. "How do you know?" He asked.

"I just got my period." My smile was so wide it could reach my ears. However, Collin didn't seem to be sharing the same emotion as he looked disappointed. "Why aren't you happy about this?" I asked him confused.

I thought he would be happy. We had forgotten to use a condom the other night and I was scared of getting pregnant. I thought he felt the same way.

"Would you be mad if I said that I wanted you to have my baby?"

I settled myself beside him and looked at him. "You really want that?" I asked him surprised.

"Of course I want that, beautiful. I love you. I can't imagine myself with anyone else."

My lips turned upwards in a smile. "I love you too, and I would love to have your baby, but not like this." He gave me a questioning look so I decided to elaborate. "I want to be married when we do have a baby. I want our baby to have a stable home with two loving parents."

Collin nodded understandingly yet there was still a hint of disappointment in his eyes. "You're right, baby." He leaned forward and placed a soft kiss on my lips.

"Wash up and get dressed while I make you breakfast." I told him as I started to get up, but he pulled me back down to him.

"Where do you think you're going, beautiful?" He asked. "You have to finish what you started." I giggled before we engaged in an out of body experience.

#

I felt arms wrap around me as I stood by the stove cooking breakfast. I turned around and saw Collin grinning down at me.

"You look very handsome, my love." I complimented him as I straightened his tie.

"Thank you, beautiful." He said as he took a seat at the round kitchen table.I turned off the stove and placed the scrambled eggs with mushroom and toast on two plates then walked over to where Collin was sitting. I placed the plates on the table and took a seat beside him.

"This looks good." He commented before digging in. "What are you going to do today?" He asked me as he took a bite.

I shrugged. "I don't have anything planned, but I was thinking about calling Rosa. Maybe she would like to come and have lunch here if it's okay with you."

"Why wouldn't it be okay with me?" He asked confused.

"It's your home. I don't want to be inviting people over if you're not okay with it."

Collin dropped his fork and looked up at me. "When are you going to understand that this is our home?" He said softly. "I already told you, baby, you're not moving out. This is your home as much as it is mine." I nodded with a smile. "I also think that it's a great idea to invite your sister."

A few minutes after we finished eating, the doorbell rang. Collin was about to stand up when I stopped him and stood up instead. I opened the door and greeted Aaliyah, Collin's maid and Gabriel, the cook. I stepped aside and let them in then closed the door behind them and walked back to the kitchen.

Collin talked to Gabriel as I placed the empty plates in the sink.

"Oh, don't do that madam." Aaliyah told me. "It's my job."

I gave the African woman a kind smile. "It is fine, Aaliyah. I don't mind."

I turned back around and walked to Collin who was finishing up his conversation with Gabriel. He gave me a smile and held my hand as we walked to the front door.

"Do you need anything before I go, beautiful?" I shook my head with a small smile on my face as I straightened his tie again. "I have a lot of meetings today, so if I don't answer my phone, then call Lila." I nodded. "I also told Gabriel to prepare lunch for you and Rosa."

"I could have cooked something myself, or we could have just ordered something."

"No, I want to pamper you." My lips turned upwards in a smile and I stood on my tippy toes and placed a soft kiss on his lips. Collin opened the door and walked out. I stood at the door and watched him as he stepped inside the elevators and the doors closed before I walked back inside the house.

Gabriel stopped me as I was walking back to our room. "Ms. Roberts." I looked sideways at him. "Do you need something specific for today's lunch?"

I thought about what Rosa would like. "Would it be too much trouble to make pizza?"

"No, not at all" He said with a smile. "Do you need something else?" I shook my head no. "I'll do something else." He said anyways with a smile before walking back to the kitchen.

I walked to my room and picked up my phone from the night stand. I looked at the time and noticed that it was a little after eight a.m. so Rosa would have been in class. I figured I would just call her later.

#

"Es!" Rosalinda yelled happily over the phone.

"Hey, sweetie, did you get out of school?" I asked my sister.

"Yes, I'm in the car with mom."

"Oh." I said in a low voice. "I wanted to ask you if you wanted to come and have lunch at Collin's house."

"Yes, I would love to!" Rosalinda said excitedly.

I chuckled. Rosalinda had been to Collin's house only once. I hadn't seen her as much as I wanted to and I felt guilty for that, but I still talked to her every single day. "Okay, sweetie, do you want me to send you the driver to pick you up like last time?"

"Mom, can you drop me off to see Es?" She asked my mother.

I didn't hear what my mother said. I still hadn't talked to her since our fight and I felt bad about it. This was the longest I had ever spent not talking to my mom. In fact, I couldn't even remember a time when we fought. "Es" I heard Rosalinda yell through the phone.

"Yes, I'm here, sweetie."

"I was saying that mom is going to drive me to Collin's place now."

"Okay, sweetie, I'm waiting for you." I told her before hanging up.

I walked out to the kitchen where Gabriel was still cooking lunch and Aaliyah was cleaning up.

"Do you need any help?" I asked them.

Aaliyah turned to me and gave me a kind smile. "Go and sit down, my child. We have everything under control here."

I nodded hesitantly before walking out of the kitchen. I felt like a good for nothing person. I didn't do anything around the house when I used to do almost everything before. It felt weird. I wasn't used to that.

As soon as I sat down on the couch in the living room, my phone vibrated. It was a message from Collin.

'I was thinking about you. I can't wait to see you when I get home tonight. I love you.'

God, I love this man I thought to myself as I started to write my reply.

'Guess what, handsome?'

His reply came instantly. 'What?'

'I love you more than words could describe. I can't wait for you to come back home so that I can show you how much.'

I waited a few minutes until I received a reply. 'I'm in a meeting now, and I can't even think straight. That's what you do to me.'

I was writing my reply when I received another text. 'What bra color are you wearing?'

'Guess you'll have to wait and see, handsome. Love you <3.' I decided to tease him a bit, make him more eager to come back home.

I stood up from my seat when the landline rang. "Hello?" I answered.

"Ms. Roberts there is a Rosalinda Roberts here to see you."

"Yes, of course. Let her in."

"Right away, Ms. Roberts" The concierge said before hanging up.

I was so excited to see my sister. Even though I talked to her every day, it was not the same as seeing her. I missed her so much. I opened the door and waited impatiently for Rosalinda to appear. The elevator suddenly dinged and the doors opened. Rosalinda was there alright, with a huge smile on her face, but she wasn't alone.

"Mom?"

**********Remember to vote, comment, share, recommend, add 'Trixie' to your reading list, and follow. :)

Chapter 18 - Apologies and Reconciliation

"Nice home" My mother commented as she looked around Collin's living room.

After an awkward greeting between me and my mother, I ushered them inside to the living room then informed Gabriel that my guests had arrived if he needed to prepare the table before I joined them in the living room.

"Yes" I replied.

Mom turned her gaze to me. "I'm sorry, Es. I should have said something. I shouldn't have let you walk out of the house. I was selfish. I was only thinking about what I wanted." She started sobbing.

I couldn't help the sight of my mom crying. I stood up and Rosalinda scooted to the side so that I could sit between them. I hugged my mom sideways as I ran my hand up and down her back in a soothing motion.

"It's okay, mom." I cooed.

"No, what I did was not okay." She looked up at me with her tear streaked face. "But, I love your dad, Es. I really do. He promised me that he has changed." I nodded firmly. "I know what he did was unforgivable, but I want to give him a second chance." She paused for a moment before continuing. "I didn't choose him over you; I was just stunned for a moment. Everything was happening so quickly. I know it's not an excuse, but please forgive me."

"I forgive you, mom. You know I could never hate you." My mom's lips turned upwards in a smile, and before I knew it she crushed me into a hug.

"Aw... Group hug" I heard Rosalinda say as she joined in on the hug.

We heard someone clear their throat. I pulled back from the hug and looked at Gabriel who had a small smile playing on his face.

"Lunch is ready, Ms. Roberts." He informed me in a formal tone.

I nodded. "Thank you, Gabriel." He nodded then walked away. "I don't know about you, but I'm starving." I told them as I stood up.

"Me too" Rosalinda agreed as mom just chuckled.

Gabriel had made pizza just like I had wanted, but he also made Mac and cheese, chicken pot pie, and Chicken Caesar Salad. I didn't know where he had the time to do all of those dishes, but I wasn't complaining.

Rosalinda, mom, and I wasted no time as we started digging in. Once we were done, Aaliyah started picking up the empty plates while Gabriel walked in holding a yummy looking cake in his hands.

"Oh, we can't eat anymore." My mom said.

I chuckled. "Mom, with Gabriel there's always dessert."

"This is my Chocolate Coconut cake." He said proudly as he placed it on the table.

I thanked him before he walked away. Aaliyah came back and placed clean plates and utensils in front of each one of us before she as well walked back to the kitchen.

Once we were done eating, Mom and Rosalinda went back to the living room while I walked to the kitchen. I thanked Gabriel for the delicious lunch and informed him that he and Aaliyah could leave once they have finished their work. I then walked to the living room where mom and Rosalinda were talking in hushed tones.

"What are you two whispering about?" I asked them with a raised eyebrow as I sat at the couch opposite of them.

"Mom wants you to come back home."

I shook my head. "I'm not coming back home."

"You can't live here forever, Es. This is not your home."

"It is." I argued. "Collin has made me feel nothing but welcome."

My mom sighed. "Is it because of your dad?" She asked sadly.

"I admit that I still can't forgive dad for what he did. I still need time, but it's not just because of him. Like I said I'm happy here, and Collin wants me to move in permanently."

"This is a big step."

"I know, mom, but I'm ready and willing."

My mom nodded sadly. "Okay. If this is what you want then I'm not going to stand in your way. I only want to see you happy. You know that, right?"

I nodded and stood up from my seat then sat down beside my mom. "Yes, mom, I know that." I told her as I rested my head on her shoulder.

They stayed a while longer before both Rosalinda and mom decided to go back home. I started to walk them out then remembered something and quickly walked to Collin and I's bedroom. I opened the closet and brought out my purse. I got what I needed then placed the purse back inside the closet before I walked back out to the door where mom and Rosalinda were waiting for me.

"What's this?" Mom asked me confused as I handed her a wad of cash.

"Just because I moved out of the house doesn't mean that I forgot about my family." I kept my hand outstretched, waiting for mom to take the money.

"Your dad's paying for everything."

"Mom, please just take the money." I said. Mom nodded hesitantly before accepting the money. I hugged both her and Rosalinda and waited for them until they stepped inside the elevator before I closed the door.

#

"Hey, beautiful" Collin greeted me as he walked in to the living room where I was watching TV.

"Hey" I greeted him excitedly and hugged him. "How was work?" I asked him as I took his jacket and bag from him, and started walking to the bedroom as he followed.

"It was okay." I heard him say as I opened the closet, put the jacket in a copper hanger, and hung it back in the closet then placed his bag on one of the chairs in the room.

I turned around and watched him rubbing his head with the palm of his hands. I walked over to him and sat down on his laps. His arms instinctively wrapped around my waist.

"You look exhausted, babe." I commented and he nodded tiredly. I kissed his cheek then stood up from his lap. "Wash up while I heat up dinner."

He nodded and stood up from the bed while I walked out of the room and in to the kitchen. I opened the fridge and brought out the Mac and cheese, chicken pot pie, and pizza and started heating them up in the microwave. I was done by the time Collin had walked in to the kitchen.

I placed the food in front of him then opened the cupboard and brought out two plates and some utensils then placed them on the table as well. Collin and I sat down and started eating the delicious food that Gabriel had cooked.

"How was your lunch with Rosalinda?"

"It was good." I told him. "Mom came as well.""Really?" He asked me surprised as he placed a forkful of the chicken pot pie in his mouth.

"Yes, she apologized to me and asked me to move back home."

Collin stopped eating and looked at me through narrowed slits. "You're not moving out."

"I know. She already knows that, I told her."

Collin looked up at me with a smile on his face. "Good because now that I have a taste of heaven I won't be able to go back to anything less."

I couldn't help the smile that made its way to my face. "Do you want dessert?" I asked him once we finished eating. "Gabriel made a delicious Chocolate Coconut Cake."

"I do want dessert." Collin said as he leaned forward. "A different kind of dessert though."

"Mm..." I made a sound of agreement.

"What kind of dessert?" I asked him teasingly.

"If I remember correctly, a very beautiful lady promised to show me the color of her lingerie."

"Is she anyone I know?" I played along.

Collin stood up from his seat and came towards me. He scooped me up from my seat making me gasp at his surprise move. He walked us back to the bedroom and threw me on the bed making me giggle. He walked towards me like a predator stalking his prey on a hunting night, and I backed away with a teasing smile on my face.

"Come here." He ordered as he gestured with his finger.

I shook my head. "No." I gave him the most flirtatious smile I could muster.

"Do not tease me, beautiful."

"Where's the fun in that?" I asked him with a teasing smile.

Collin growled lowly before he jumped at me.

#

A couple of hours later, I was resting my head on Collin's chest as we both breathed heavily. Collin smoothed down my hair as I drew circles on his chest.

"My energy's drained out. I don't feel like putting my clothes on."

"Why would you put your clothes on? There's no better way than to sleep naked." He said seriously as he placed a kiss at the top of my head.

I chuckled and stood up from the bed and started walking towards the bathroom to take a shower and freshen up. However, Collin did not follow. I turned sideways and looked at him.

"Coming?"

He didn't need further invitation as he jumped off the bed and walked before me to the bathroom.

As soon as we finished our shower, Collin lay down on the bed to sleep while I started dressing to go to work. I couldn't help but notice the frown on Collin's face.

"What's wrong, handsome?" I asked him as I raised my hands to put on my dress.

"Nothing" He grumbled.

I sat at the edge of the bed and strapped on my heels then walked over to Collin and sat beside where he was laying. "What's wrong, babe?" I asked him as I smoothed back his hair.

"Nothing" He grumbled again and turned to the other side so that I wouldn't be able to see his face.

I sighed and pressed a kiss on his cheek. "I'll be back as usual." I informed him. "I love you." I didn't get a reply and I didn't think that I would.

I stood up from the bed and walked to the door. I held the door handle in my hand and turned back to look at Collin. I could see his face from where I was standing and he looked at me with anger, sadness, and hurt in his eyes; all at the same time. I sighed once more before I opened the door and walked out.

**********Remember to vote, comment, share, recommend, add 'Trixie' to your reading list, and follow. :)

Chapter 19 - Fighting and Reconciling

I opened my eyes to the sun peeking through the curtains, hitting my side of the bed. I looked to the side at Collin and found him with his eyes open looking up at the ceiling.

"Good morning." I scooted closer to him and rested my head on his chest.

He didn't reply nor did his hands come around me like they used to whenever I was close to him.

I looked up at him through my lashes. "Are you okay?"

He looked down at me for a second, but didn't say anything before his gaze went back up to the ceiling. What was his problem? I thought to myself.

Adamant to make him smile at least, I removed the duvet from his body and straddled his waist. I kissed my way from his lips down to his neck and chest. I felt him growing harder so I knew he was reacting to my touch, but there was no groan or moan, nothing. He had his poker face on. I scratched him lightly along his sides with my nails knowing that he liked that, but I didn't get the reaction I wanted either. I knew that his body was reacting to my touches, but it was clear that he didn't want to act on them.

"Okay, what's wrong?" I asked as I sat up straight.

Collin looked at me, but no words came out of his mouth. I sighed.

"Collin, please talk to me. I want to know if I did something wrong."

"I don't want you to work at the strip club again."

I groaned and flopped down on the bed beside him. "Not again!"

"Didn't you ask me what's wrong?" He looked at me through narrowed eyes. "I'm telling you what's wrong."

"I'm tired of having this fight, Collin."

"I'm also tired of men ogling your body while I just sit back with my hands folded, unable to do anything."

I sat up straight on the bed and looked at him. "Why did you ask me out then? You knew I was a stripper, or maybe you just thought of me as a piece of ass?"

Collin sat up straight and looked at me through narrowed eyes. "You know very well that you were never a piece of ass to me." His tone was dangerously calm, sending chills down my spine.

I had never seen him this way, and honestly it scared me. I stood up from the bed and started walking to the bathroom when I felt my arm being pulled back. I looked sideways at Collin and noticed that he was seething. "I'm not done yet."

"I don't want to talk about it!" I told him angrily as I tried to pull my arm back, but he had a strong hold on it.

"You will do as I say and leave your job!"

"I am not your slave and I will do as I please."

His hold on my arm was getting tighter. "Do not test me, Esmeralda."

His hold on my arm had become unbearable. My eyes brimmed with tears and the corner of my mouth was twitching rapidly. Collin probably noticed because he released his hold on my arm. His face softened as he noticed the slight bruise he had left behind, but it was gone as soon as it came. Without a word, he walked out of the room and slammed the door behind him. I let the tears fall down freely down my face. My arm was hurting me and I couldn't get the way Collin talked to me out of my head. This was not the Collin I loved. This was a completely different person; a stranger. I wiped the tears with the back of my hands and walked in to the bathroom.

As I walked out of the bathroom, I saw Collin getting dressed for work. Neither one of us said a word to each other as I walked to my side of the bed and sat down at the edge with my back to him. I heard Collin shuffling around the room before he walked out and closed the door shut with force.

#

I stood in the kitchen as I heated up some dinner for Collin. He was supposed to be home in a short while. He hadn't contacted me all day and neither did I. I wasn't mad at him because as soon as the anger started to simmer down, I started to feel the hurt from the way he talked to me and the way he treated me. However, I knew he would be exhausted and hungry when he arrived home so I decided to heat him up some dinner.

I brought the Chicken Cordon Bleu out of the microwave and placed it on the kitchen table then mixed the salad before placing it on the table as well. I placed a glass of water beside them, then walked to the bedroom. I stripped off my clothes and put on my pajamas then walked to the bathroom to brush my teeth before going to the spare bedroom. I was definitely not sleeping in Collin's room.

I lay on the bed and looked up the ceiling. I needed to talk to someone. I picked up my phone from the nightstand and pressed Rosalinda's number then hit the call button.

"Es!" She answered happily.

"Hey, sweetie"

"I miss you." Excitement was clear in her tone.

"Me too" I told her honestly. My tone was sad and that did not go unnoticed by Rosalinda. She knew me very well.

"What's wrong, Es?" She sounded worried.

"Nothing, Rosa. I'm just a little tired."

"Are you lying to me?" She asked me in an accusing tone.

I chuckled. "Are you calling me a liar?"

"Me? Pfft... no!" She said in a sarcastic tone and we both fell into fits of laughter. Suddenly, dad's voice sounded in the background. "I need to go, Es. Dinner's ready."

"Okay, sweetie, I'll talk to you later."

"Love you."

"Love you too, Rosa." I hung up and placed the phone back on the nightstand.

I sighed and turned off the lamp beside my bed then pulled the duvet up to my chin. As soon as I closed my eyes shut, I heard the front door opening. I didn't move knowing it was Collin.

Several minutes later, I heard footsteps outside of my door then light entered as Collin opened the door and stepped inside. I closed my eyes not wanting to deal with him. I felt him sit down on the bed as the mattress squished down.

"Es" He called my name softly. I kept my eyes closed. "Es, are you asleep?" He asked again, but I still kept my eyes closed. I heard him sigh. "I'm sorry, Es. I really am." He said in a low voice and I felt him starting to stand up.

I opened my eyes and grabbed his hand stopping him. He turned to me with a guilty look on his face. We looked at each other for a moment before I broke the silence.

"Stay."

"Are you sure?" He asked me and I nodded. He kicked off his shoes and lay down on the bed beside me. He put his arm around me and pulled me closer to him.

"I'm sorry, Es. I didn't mean to be harsh on you this morning, but I just go crazy every time I think how other men grow tents in their pants as they gawk at you."

I looked up at him. "Collin, we need to work through this. We can't keep having the same fight all the time."

"I know." He said disheartened. "Why can't you quit?"

"I need the money, Collin. I have already told you that."

"I'll give you whatever you want." There was a slight pleading to his tone which was completely unlike him.

"I don't want your money, Collin. I never did."

He sighed sadly. "Then why can't you work some other job where men don't stare at your naked body?"

I took a deep breath before responding. "Stripping pays more." Collin didn't say anything and I knew he didn't know what to say. I turned so that I was lying on my stomach and placed the palm of my hand on his cheek. "I know that it pains you to see me go to work every single night while you're here helpless, unable to stop all the stares, but don't think of it that way." Collin looked at me questioningly. "All the men get to look at me, yes, but you my handsome man get to touch me."

"That is true." He agreed with a smirk.

"I love you, Collin." I placed a soft kiss on his lips.

"I love you too, Esmeralda." I gave him a smile. "I'm sorry I made you cry today. I feel bad that I am the one that made those beautiful eyes fill up with tears."

"You heard me cry?" I asked him surprised.

"Yes, I was standing behind the door." He told me then caressed my face. "I am so sorry, beautiful." I nodded letting him know that it's okay. "Come on; let's go back to our room."

We stood form the bed and walked out of the room when I asked him. "Did you have dinner?" He shook his head no. "Come, let's have dinner first." I hooked my arm with his and rested my head on his shoulder as we walked out to the kitchen.

"You prepared dinner for me even though you were mad at me?" He asked me as he saw the food atop of the kitchen table.

"I knew you would be exhausted and hungry." He gave me a wide smile and kissed my lips.

#

Collin's fork stopped midway through his mouth as he settled his gaze on the dark purple bruise on my arm that he had left on me earlier that morning. I pulled my short sleeves pajama top down trying to cover it up. Collin placed his fork back down on the plate with a bang.

"Did I do that?"

I didn't reply and casted my eyes downwards. Collin stood up from his seat and walked up to me. He bent down in front of me and held my arm softly as he checked the bruise he had left.

"I'm so sorry, baby. I'm so sorry." He apologized as he placed soft kisses on the bruise as if trying to make it go away.

I held his face in my hands and looked straight into his guilt-stricken eyes. "It is okay, Collin. It will get better in a couple of days."

"I am so sorry." He apologized again.

"Collin, I'm fine." I said softly and crashed my lips to his in a sensual kiss.

Just then his phone rang. I grabbed it from the table and handed it to him.

"Hello?" He answered his eyes still trained on me. "Yes, okay." There was a slight pause. "We'll be there." He hung up and looked at me.

"Mom invited us on Sunday for lunch. The whole family is going to be there. I told her we will be there, but if you don't want to go I can cancel."

I shook my head with a smile on my face. "I would love to go."

I captured his lips with mine in an explicit come-and-get-me kiss then stood up and walked to the bedroom knowing that he was right behind me.

**********Remember to vote, comment, share, recommend, add 'Trixie' to your reading list, and follow. :)

Chapter 20 - Past Relationship

"Are you ready, beautiful?" Collin asked me as he walked in to the bedroom.

"I'm almost done, babe." He nodded and sat down on the bed as he watched me apply my makeup.

A few minutes later, I placed the lipstick that I had used back on the vanity mirror table, stood up from my seat, and turned around so that I was facing Collin.

"You look beautiful." He stood up from the bed and walked towards me. He wrapped his arms around my waist and pulled me closer to him. "Very beautiful" He murmured as he dipped his head down for kiss, but I pulled back.

"Lipstick, babe" I raised my index finger in warning.

"Such a tease" He grumbled and I chuckled as he released his arms from around my waist then held my hand and started walking us out.

#

Collin rang the doorbell and we waited for someone to open the door. He squeezed my hand and I looked up at him. He had the most loving smile on his face.

The door suddenly opened, and the maid greeted us then ushered us inside the house. We could hear the sounds of chattering and laughter as we approached the living room.

"Well, would you look who's here?" We heard a voice from behind us say and turned around.

Benjamin, Collin's brothers, stood there with a wide grin on his face.

"Hey, pretty lady." He took my hand and placed a kiss there.

Collin growled lowly making our gaze shift to him. I felt Benjamin release his hand from mine and from the corner of my eyes saw him as he raised his hands in mock surrender. I chuckled as Collin pulled me to his side possessively. We all walked to the living room where it was crowded.

"Who are all those people?" I whispered in his ear.

"Family" Collin replied.

I watched as Margaret, Collin's mother, walked towards us with a happy smile on her face. She hugged Collin first before pulling me into her arms.

"I'm so glad you came." She told me as she pulled back.

"I'm happy to be here." I said honestly.

Just then Silas, Collin's father, approached us as well. "Hey, son" He patted Collin on his shoulder then looked at me. "How are you, Esmeralda."

"I'm good." I answered politely.

"Let me introduce you to our extended family." Margaret said eagerly.

Collin and I followed her as she introduced me to a couple of the extended family. Eventually the maid announced that lunch was served, and we all went in to the dining room. Collin sat on one side of me while Benjamin sat on the other side. The dining room was filled with noise and laughter. I looked up at Collin who was engaged in a conversation with a man beside him.

"Aren't you going to eat?" Benjamin whispered to me. I looked up at him and nodded with a smile then held my fork and dug into the salad.

"So, Esmeralda, what do you work?" A woman across of me on the table asked. I didn't know who she was since I didn't get introduced to everyone.

I suddenly froze in place; my fork midway through my mouth. Collin's parents didn't ask me what I worked and I was very grateful for that. The whole room went silent as they all looked at me waiting for me to reply.

"Esmeralda works as a bartender." Collin piped up as he squeezed my thigh.

"Oh." The woman said looking unimpressed then continued eating as did everyone else.

I looked up at Collin and silently thanked him. I didn't want people knowing that I was a stripper. It was not something I wanted to share with people that I had just met. Collin squeezed my thigh once more in reassurance.

"Thank you." I murmured. He leaned forward and pressed a soft kiss on my cheek.

Everyone scattered around the living room and garden once we finished lunch. Collin and I were sitting in the living room when his uncle walked with him to the garden to talk in some business related stuff. I stayed back in the living room and started to write a text message to Rosalinda when I felt someone sit beside me.

"Why are you alone?"

I turned to the side and smiled when I saw that it was Benjamin. "Collin just went out to the garden with your uncle."

"Oh." Benjamin nodded. "Are you having fun?" He asked me.

I nodded with a smile. "Yeah"

"It doesn't seem like it though." He commented with a grin.

I chuckled. "I don't know everyone here and I'm not the type to mingle."

Benjamin nodded understandingly. He sat with me and kept me company for a while. He was a really funny man, and I felt myself completely at ease with him.

"No way!" I laughed even harder.

"Wait there's more." Benjamin said. "He threw his pajama pants out and mom never found out."

By this point I was in full blown laughter. Benjamin was telling me about a time when young Collin watched a horror movie at home with his family, and peed in his pants. His mom asked him about it and he said that he accidently threw water on himself.

I looked outside at the garden and saw Collin talking to a strikingly beautiful lady. She had her hand on his arm and was standing so close to him.

"Who are you looking at?" Benjamin asked me as he followed my gaze.

"Who is she?" I asked him. Surprisingly, I didn't sound angry just curious.

"That's Sienna, Collin's ex." Benjamin probably noticed the questioning expression on my face then said. "You didn't know."

I looked at him and shook my head. "I figured he had a long list of ex girlfriends, but we never really talked about it." Benjamin nodded, but didn't say anything. "Did he love her?" I asked him as I looked back at them. She was caressing his cheek in such a loving manner. I felt like an intruder looking at a private moment between two lovers. I turned my gaze back to Benjamin who just nodded his head.

"I'm not going to lie. They loved each other very much and were engaged for a short while, but they left abruptly. No one knew why, and Collin refused to talk about it." I nodded sadly. "You shouldn't worry though." He tried to assure me. "It's clear how much Collin loves you. "

I was silent for a few seconds before I asked. "Can you show me to the bathroom?" Benjamin nodded and led me to the downstairs bathroom.

I turned on the water and washed my hands then just stood there for a moment to breathe before I opened the door and walked out. I found Collin waiting for me outside of the bathroom. How did he know where I was?

"Ben told me you were here." He answered my unasked question. "Are you okay?" He asked me. "You look a little pale." He held my face and looked at me worriedly.

I gave him a small reassuring smile. "I'm fine." I said softly.

He nodded. "I wanted to see if you wanted to go home."

"Yes, sure" I agreed. "Let's say goodbye to your parents first."

We went out to the garden where his parents were at and we said our goodbyes to them before we went back to Collin's penthouse. As soon as we arrived at the penthouse, I walked to our room with Collin on my heels. I started undressing to put on my loungewear when I felt Collin's arms around my waist.

"I'm tired, Collin." I released myself from his hold and walked in to the bathroom.

#

Once I finished preparing dinner, I walked to Collin's home office where he had been holed up since we came back from his parents' house. I knocked on the door softly.

"Come in."

I opened the door slightly and poked my head inside. "Dinner's ready."

He nodded firmly. "I'll be out in a minute." I nodded and closed the door then headed back to the kitchen.

I placed the food on the table and sat down as I waited for Collin to arrive. A minute later, he arrived and sat down on the table. We ate our dinner silently, only the sound of utensils clacking was heard. Collin suddenly placed his fork and knife down, and looked at me.

"Are you mad at me, Es?" His voice was soft and hesitating.

I placed my fork down as well and looked at him. "No, why would I be mad at you?"

"Ever since we came back from lunch you've been distant with me."

"I saw you." My tone was soft, and not angry.

"I don't get you."

"I saw you with your ex fiancée." I elaborated. "You were really getting touchy with each other." I don't know how I was still calm.

"Sienna?" I nodded.

"Do you still love her?" I asked him. "I won't be mad at you, I just want to know."

"Baby, Sienna was my ex fiancée, yes, and I did love her, yes, but all the love was gone when I found her sleeping with another man."

I looked at him wide eyed. "She cheated on you?" I asked him disbelievingly, and he just nodded. "Why was she at your parents' house if she is not family?"

"My parents are close friends with hers so they get invited to pretty much everything."

"So we'll be seeing a lot more of her." I said dejectedly.

"Not necessarily."

"Why did she have her hands all over you?" I asked him in a low voice,

Collin stood up from his seat and squatted down in front of me. "She wanted me back, but I told her that I didn't because I was with the most beautiful girl."

"You told her that?" I asked him with a small smile.

"Well, not really." He shook his head making me chuckle. "I told her that I was with a stunning woman."

"Liar" I chuckled and wrapped my arms around his neck.

"Are we okay, beautiful?" He asked me as he pulled back, and I nodded. "I love you, baby, I don't want you to ever forget that."

"I love you too, Collin." I told him honestly as I looked lovingly into his beautiful eyes.

**********Remember to vote, comment, share, recommend, add 'Trixie' to your reading list, and follow. :)

Chapter 21 - Unexpected, but Pleasant Surprise

"Good morning, beautiful." I heard Collin say from behind me as I was pouring coffee into our mugs.

I held both mugs in my hand and turned around to face him. "Good morning, handsome." I stood on my tippy toes and pressed a soft kiss on his lips then walked to the kitchen table and placed the mugs beside the Greek Yogurt Parfait and scrambled eggs I had prepared.

Collin and I sat on the table and started eating our breakfast. My phone suddenly started ringing. I looked at the screen and noticed that it was my dad calling. I left it ringing and continued eating my food like nothing had happened.

"Who is calling you this early in the morning?" Collin questioned me.

"My dad" I answered as I put a spoonful of the delicious yogurt parfait in my mouth.

"Well, aren't you going to answer him?" He asked me with a raised eyebrow.

I placed the spoon down and looked at him. "No, of course not" I said in a matter-of-fact tone.

Collin sighed and looked at me. "Es, baby, you can't keep ignoring your dad. I know that he left you when you needed him, but what's done is done. Right now you are given a second chance to reconcile with him and make things better so why not take it?"

"You just don't understand it, Collin. You have lived the perfect life. You don't know what it feels like for someone you love to leave you." I raised my voice.

"I'm not saying that I understand it." I could see him trying to control his anger. "Your mom and sister forgave him. I don't see why you can't."

"I just can't, okay?" I stood up from my seat and held the parfait bowl in my hand then walked to the sink.

Collin's breath tickled the back of my neck making the hair rise. "I'm sorry, Es. I didn't mean to make you mad."

I turned around and looked at his sorrowful expression. "It's fine. I didn't mean to get all worked up either. It's just that I don't like to talk about my dad."

"Okay, I won't talk about him anymore unless you do." He promised.

"Thank you, babe, that's all I ask." I stood on my tippy toes and placed a soft kiss on his lips.

#

"Conner wants to see you." One of the dancers told me as she walked into the dressing room.

I placed my makeup brush down and stood up from my seat then walked out of the dressing room and made my way towards Conner's office. I knocked once before the door opened. Conner seemed to be in a good mood as he had a grin on his face.

"You asked to see me?"

"Yes." He grinned even more as he walked back behind his table and sat down on his chair. "You have a private dance to perform."

"How much did they pay?" I asked him, finally figuring out why that grin couldn't be wiped off his face.

"You get one thousand five hundred dollars." He stood up from his seat and walked towards me then handed me the money.

"How much did you get?" I asked him as I nodded my head towards him.

"Five hundred dollars" I was impressed that I had gotten the larger sum, but then again I had to admit that Connor was a fair man.

I nodded. "Which room?"

I walked towards the room that my client was waiting for me at. I nodded at the bodyguard and he opened the door, letting me in. The room was somewhat dark so I couldn't see what my client's face looked like. All I hoped was he wouldn't be some greasy, smelly man who couldn't keep his hands to himself.

I could see the client gesturing with his fingers for me to come closer. I walked slowly towards him and gasped with pleasure once I could clearly see the face of my mystery client.

"I heard you wanted a dance." I told Collin seductively.

"You heard right, beautiful." I walked closer to him and placed a kiss on his lips. "Now, dance for me." He ordered smugly.

"Your wish is my command, sir." I purred in his ear as I turned around and strode away from him.

I placed one foot directly in front of the other, and dragged my feet in a come-hither effect. I glided my fingertips up and down my body then stroked my neck and collarbone, smoothly and lightly. My hands went down to the dress I had on, and I started tugging on it. I then bent down and grazed my hands down the front of my leg. Still in that position, I started to take off my dress, but instead of removing it all the way, I left it rolled around my wrists. Twisting my right hand once, I created a loose handcuff. I rose back up and lifted my hands over my head. After a moment, I flung the dress at Collin. I caught Collin's gaze and saw him sitting forward with the dress in his hands. He raised it to his nose and smelled it. I could feel him getting excited. I twirled a lock of my hair around my finger then flipped it to the side. My fingers went to the straps of my bra as I started playing with it. I teased Collin for a few seconds until I heard him groan. I chuckled as my hands went behind me and I unsnapped the bra letting my breasts fall freely. I placed my hands on my breasts and started massaging them erotically.

"Don't cover them up." Collin told me.

"I'm not, babe." I assured him. "I'm just giving you a show to remember." I smirked.

I stood with my feet slightly apart, threw my shoulders back, put my hands on my knees, and circled my butt around. I turned my head trying to look at Collin and I knew that he liked what he was seeing. I decided to tease him even more and got down on my hands and knees then slid onto my stomach. Once I was on my stomach, I flipped onto my back, extended my arms straight out on the ground over my head and lifted my legs up in the air. I crossed them at the ankle, fluttered my legs, opened into a straddle-style split facing him then I slowly caressed my v-zone while looking straight into his eyes. Even through the loud music, I could hear him hiss. Pleased with his reaction, I smirked and rolled over onto all fours, sat back on my feet then stood up one leg at a time and walked slowly towards him. I placed both of my hands on either side of his lap for support and lifted my right leg in the air before placing in over his lap, and did the same to the left then grinded against him. His hands went to my breasts, caressing them and giving them the attention they desperately needed. I looked at him and saw the want and need in his eyes. I kept on grinding against him and I felt him growing harder. My hands went to his hair as I tugged on it. Suddenly he held my waist; stopping me from grinding into him anymore.

"You're going to give me blue balls, baby." I chuckled and started to stand up when he pulled me back down to him. "Stay here a little longer."

I shrugged. "Sure. You already paid more than you're supposed to." I winked.

#

As soon as Collin opened the door to his penthouse, he pushed me against the wall and started kissing me hungrily, ravishing me with his mouth. His hands roamed all over my body as he started tugging on my dress. We pulled away from the kiss just for a second as I raised my hands over my head and he pulled the dress up and threw it on the floor. His hands then went behind me as he unsnapped my bra and threw it on the floor as well. I started to fumble with the buttons on his shirt, and was starting to get impatient.

"To hell with it" I mumbled as I tore his shirt and the buttons went flying all over the place.

Collin looked at me with surprise and amusement in his eyes. "Do you know how much this shirt cost me?" He asked teasingly.

"You're rich. You can get another one." I said seriously as I jumped up and wrapped my legs around his waist.

He held me tightly against him and crashed his lips against mine then walked us to the bedroom. He kicked the door open with his leg then threw me on the bed. I giggled as I watched him hastily remove his trousers and boxers before joining me on the bed. He crashed his lips against mine in an intense and intoxicating kiss then suddenly pulled back. I whined wanting more of him.

"All good things come to those who wait, beautiful." He said with a smirk as he slid down and wrapped his fingers around the waistband of my pants and pulled them down then his head disappeared between my thighs.

"Oh, oh" I arched my back off the bed and ran my hand through Collin's hair, pulling at it roughly. "Oh god, Collin"

Collin looked up at me for a moment before he went back to pleasuring me. I couldn't take it anymore and just fell apart.

"That was..." I trailed off as Collin came back up. I turned around so that I was on top of him and wrapped my hand around his hardness as I began to stroke him. Collin groaned and pulled his head back.

"Oh, god, that feels good." He placed his hands on either side of his head.

I dipped my head down and licked the head as I looked up at his reaction. He seemed to like it so I licked it some more before I released my hands from around him and wrapped my lips around his shaft. I took him slowly until he was deep inside my mouth.

"Oh, Es" He groaned. "I'm going to come." He held my face in his hands. "Come up to me." I did as told and he kissed me roughly on my lips. "You are amazing." He complimented before ordering. "On all fours"

I did as told and looked to the side as I watched him position himself behind me before thrusting hard inside me. I felt the air leaving my lungs. Collin moved in and out so roughly. We had never done it that way before, but I had to admit that I kind of like it. The sound of skin slapping against each other was so loud. I clutched the sheets tightly in my hands as Collin pulled my hair back and increased his pace. Suddenly, I felt a smack on my ass bringing me apart in no time, and Collin followed soon after as he flopped down on me before shifting his weight so he was resting beside me.

"That was... intense." I said breathlessly as I looked sideways at him.

"Did I hurt you?" He asked me concerned.

I shook my head no. "I actually like it."

"Is that so?" He asked amused.

"Mm..." I nodded. "Round two?" I asked him.

Collin chuckled before flipping me on my stomach and getting down to business.

**********Remember to vote, comment, share, recommend, add 'Trixie' to your reading list, and follow. :)

Chapter 22 - The Confrontation

"Would you like me to cook something specific today, Ms. Roberts?" Gabriel asked politely.

I shook my head with a small smile on my face. "Anything would be fine." I said honestly. Gabriel nodded then started preparing what he wanted to cook while I continued mixing the ingredients for the cheesecake I was going to prepare.

I didn't feel comfortable with people doing things for me, but Collin wouldn't have it, saying that he wanted to pamper me. I felt so useless so I decided to make him a dessert at least.

Lost in thought, I didn't hear my phone ringing, until Aaliyah came forward holding the phone in her hand.

"Here you go, madam."

I wiped my hands on my jeans before taking the phone from her hands. "Thank you, Aaliyah."

I looked at the screen and noticed that my dad was the one calling. I placed the phone in the counter and let it go to voicemail as I continued my work.

A couple of hours later, I heard the landline ringing so I ran to the living room to pick it up.

"Hello?"

"Ms. Roberts, Your mom is here. Should I let her up?" The concierge asked me.

Weird, my mom didn't call me or tell me that she was coming. I shrugged.

"Yes, of course."

The doorbell rang as I was removing the cheesecake from the oven.

"Should I get it?" Aaliyah asked me.

I nodded. "Yes, please."

I placed the cheesecake on the kitchen table to let it cool a bit then removed my cooking mitts before walking out to the living room.

"Hey, sweetheart" My mom stood up from her seat with open arms, but I was rooted to my spot; unable to move as I looked at my dad.

"What are you doing here?" My tone was harsh.

Dad stood up and looked at me with a sad and helpless expression. "I came to see you, baby girl."

"Did you think that maybe I didn't want to see you?" I asked him with a raised eyebrow, trying to keep my cool.

"Es, you can't keep ignoring you father, please." Mom's eyes were pleading, and I knew how hard it was for her to see her family shattered.

"Es, please all I'm asking for is a second chance." My dad pleaded.

"A second chance?" I scoffed. "Why so you could leave us again?"

Dad sighed and ran his hand through his hair while mom just looked at me disapprovingly.

"I did a mistake once; I promise you that it won't happen again."

I shook my head. "No. You did it once, you'll do it again. I won't stand by and watch you leave us again."

"This is enough!" My mom suddenly yelled. "Your father came here asking for your forgiveness. Don't be a brat, Esmeralda. I raised you better than that!"

I was shocked by my mom's sudden outburst. It was like she had all those emotions bottled up inside of her and boom went her calmness.

"So I'm now considered a brat because I'm looking out for my family's wellbeing?" I raised my voice.

"No one asked you to." My mom argued, equally exasperated.

"You're right, no one asked me to!" I yelled. "But when good ol' dad here decided he was better off alone." I pointed my hand at my dad. "I had no option other than to take that responsibility."

"I already said I'm sorry." My dad was raising his voice now as well, clearly angry.

"Yeah, well guess what?" I looked at him through narrowed eyes. "Sorry doesn't do it anymore."

Just then I heard the front door opening and closing, and saw Collin striding my way.

"Is everything okay?" He asked me as he snaked his arm around my waist while his eyes were trained on my parents.

"Everything's fine, Collin" my mom answered softly.

"No, everything is not fine." I argued. "You left us when we needed you most and that is not okay. Waltzing back into our lives unannounced and expecting our forgiveness is also not okay." I yelled as my body started shaking. With anger.

Collin looked at me with concern in his eyes. He held me tightly against his body as if trying to protect me. "Mr. and Mrs. Roberts, please it is best if you just leave now." I looked at mom's betrayed expression and dad's forlorn one.

"I did not raise you to be a grudge-bearing and resentful person." My mom spoke her thoughts.

I stayed quiet and didn't reply back because I knew if I did, we would start fighting all over again, and I didn't want that. I was thankful for Collin being at my side at that moment because I could barely stand on my two feet.

Mom and dad started walking out of the living room and I couldn't help but feel bad about what had happened. I wasn't what mom had called me. I wasn't a grudge-bearing and resentful person.

"Mom" I called out. Both mom and dad turned around and looked at me expectantly. "I'm not what you said, mom." I told her softly. "I'm just looking out for the people I love." I turned my gaze towards my dad. "I don't hate you either, dad. I hated what you did to us. I just need some time."

He nodded as a hopeful smile made its way to his face before they both turned back around and walked out.

Collin kept his arm around my waist and led me to the couch behind us. He helped me sit down and held my face in his hands. "Are you okay, beautiful?"

I nodded. "I will be." I assured him. I then noticed that it was still early for Collin to be home. "Why are you here early?"

"The concierge called me and informed me that your parents were here."

My eyebrows furrowed together. "Why did he call and tell you?"

"I asked him to."

I backed away a bit from his hold. "I don't understand."

"The concierge reports to me about everything that happens and everyone that comes in when I'm not around."

I looked at him incredulously. "So you're keeping tabs on me?"

"It's for your safety." He said softly.

"I cannot believe you." I stood up from my seat and walked to the bedroom. This was too much for me.

Collin followed me to the bedroom and closed the door behind him. "Es, baby, I'm doing this for our safety."

"What? Is the mafia on your tracks?" I laughed humourlessly as I took a seat on the bed.

Collin looked at me seriously and he didn't look impressed with my sarcastic comment. "I have a lot of competitors, and you'd be amazed at the things people would do." I kept quiet as I listened to him. "I also have to admit that it's because I get jealous as well." He gave me a guilty look as he sat down beside me.

"Why would you get jealous?" I asked him with a shrug.

Collin looked at me with a look that said 'you're crazy'. "You are the most beautiful woman I have ever met." The sincerity could be heard in his tone. "You may be oblivious to it, but you don't see how men look at you."

My cheeks flushed at his confession. "Maybe that's true, but I'm yours."

"I know that, but I still can't help the feeling that you might eventually realize that you can do better than me and leave."

I looked at this man in front of me. He was not the confident, self-assured man I knew. This one looked like a small boy wanting to be accepted, wanting to be loved. Suddenly, it clicked.

"Collin, I'm not Sienna." His ex fiancée had obviously left a bad mark in his life for him to feel insecure around the person he loved. Collin looked at me through sad eyes. He broke my heart. I held his face in my hands and lay it on my lap. I started smoothing his hair mindlessly. "Collin, honey, I don't know Sienna, but I can assure you that she isn't a smart girl because no girl with her right mind would want to leave someone like you." I bent down and placed a soft kiss on his head then continued smoothing his hair. "I love you, Collin. I love you so much, and I would never even think about cheating on you." I paused for a moment. "I know you might find it hard to believe, but I want you to have faith in me, in us."

Collin was silent, but I knew that he heard me. At that moment, I didn't feel hatred towards anyone as much as I felt hatred towards Sienna for causing emotional damage to the man I love.

**********Remember to vote, comment, share, recommend, add 'Trixie' to your reading list, and follow. :)

Chapter 23 - Background Check

I woke up to soft feather-like kisses on my skin. I squirmed in my spot and opened one eye. My silk night gown was gathered just below my breasts as Collin placed kisses all over my naked belly, and blew cool breaths after every kiss. I closed my eye shut and relished in the feeling.

"I know you're awake, beautiful." Collin said and I giggled then opened both of my eyes. "I made you breakfast."

Just then my tummy grumbled making my cheeks burn in embarrassment while Collin just chuckled.

"Come on." He held my hand and we stood up from the bed and walked towards the small coffee table where Collin had placed a tray of yummy looking breakfast.

"Go ahead and start before me." I told him. "I need to use the bathroom." He nodded and sat down while I walked in to the bathroom.

"You cooked this?" I asked him once I walked out of the bathroom and sat down beside him; referring to the waffles and bananas, French toast with strawberry jam, and oatmeal with apricots and raisins.

Collin nodded. I looked at him impressed. "I can cook, baby, I just don't have the time." He explained.

We ate our breakfast and talked a bit. I was happy that Collin was feeling better. After our conversation the day before, he told me he does have faith in us, but he was just scared. This was a feeling that was going to be hard for him to let go of, but he would try his best. I silently vowed to show him how much I love him every single day and prove to him that not every woman is like Sienna.

I looked at Collin as he ate his waffle heartily. God, how much I loved this man. Collin probably noticed my eyes on him because he looked at me questioningly.

"Are you okay?" He asked me.

I nodded with a small smile on my face then placed my hand on his lap and rubbed it up and down his thigh. "I love you."

Collin's lips turned upwards in a sincere smile. "I love you too." He interlaced his hand with the one on his lap an raised it up to his lips.

#

"Come in." I opened the door and walked in to Collin's home office. He had been so swamped with work and kept himself holed up in his home office.

"Dinner's ready, babe." I informed him as I walked towards him. Collin turned his chair sideways and I sat down on his lap. My arms instinctively went around his neck as his went around my waist. "You're always holed up here. What are you working on anyways?"

"I'm trying to find a solution for a problem that occurred at work." He informed me vaguely.

"Can I help?" I asked him. I really wanted to help him if I could.

Collin smiled and shook his head no. "Let's go eat, baby."

My eyes went to the papers scattered over his desk and something caught my eye. I released my arms from around Collin's neck and stood up. He held my hand in his and we both walked out of his home office.

I kept thinking about the paper I saw in Collin's office. I wanted to make sure that my eyes weren't just making me see things.

"I'll be right back, babe. I need to use the bathroom." Collin nodded with a small smile before he resumed eating his dinner.

I stood up from the table and walked back to Collin's home office. I opened the door slowly and walked behind his desk. My eyes were about to pop out of its socket as I saw the papers; I wasn't mistaken. I glanced through the paper and was shocked at what I was seeing.

Just then I heard Collin's footsteps coming, but I was too shocked to even react or place the paper back down.

"There you are. I thought..." Collin trailed off as he noticed the paper in my hand. He came closer towards me and saw the contents. "Fuck." He muttered under his breath. "I can explain."

I looked at him. "Explain what, Collin? How you did a background check on the woman you claim to love?"

"You don't understand, Es." He pleaded with his eyes.

"Enlighten me then." I looked at him with a daring look.

Collin sighed and ran his hand through his hair before he spoke. "I wanted to know more about you."

I laughed humorlessly. "Have you ever heard of asking?"

"I always ask you, but you never seem to give me an answer. I asked you time and time again why you can't leave your job at the strip club and all you give me is some vague answer about how you need the money."

I sat down on his desk chair and placed the paper down. "Did you get your answer?" I asked him appalled. "Did you finally figure out what is the real reason that I work as a stripper?"

Collin had the audacity to look away embarrassedly as he spoke. "If you would have told me about Rosa's cancer, I would have gladly helped out financially."

"I don't want your money!" I told him exasperated. "I am very capable of getting my own money."

"And losing your dignity along the way" He muttered under his breath.

"What was that?" I asked him threateningly.

"This is not a dignified profession. If it was, you wouldn't be ashamed of it. You wouldn't have a problem telling my parents what you do for a living."

"You think I don't know that?" I yelled angrily. "You think I enjoy what I do?"

"Then quit!" his tone of voice matching mine. "I am more than willing to cover all the expenses!"

"I don't want your money." I said each word with force trying to make a point. "What you did is an invasion of privacy." My tone was angry. Collin didn't reply nor did he look at me. I suddenly remembered something. "Meeting you at the supermarket that day wasn't a coincidence, was it?" I asked him referring to the first time we bumped into each other at the supermarket. I was surprised that time when I saw him because rarely did someone outside of the neighborhood go in, and especially not someone as Collin.

Collin rubbed the back of his neck with his hand. "Actually that was another background check." I opened my mouth to speak, but he was faster than me. "It was a basic information type of thing."

I laughed humorlessly. "What happened to the traditional 'I would like to know more about you'" I mocked a man's voice.

"I'm not good with the traditional pleasantries."

I scoffed at his response. "So you decided to do a background check on me."

Collin sighed. "Please don't be mad at me, Es." He outstretched his hand to touch my cheek, but I backed away. I could see the hurt in his eyes, but I shrugged it away.

"I feel exposed." I told him tiredly.

Collin bent down on his knees in front of me and placed his hands on my lap. "I did what I did because I wanted to get to know you more. I didn't do it to use the information against you. I know I didn't go by it the traditional way, but please don't hold it against me. You know my intentions are good."

I sighed as I looked at Collin's crestfallen expression. What he did was absolutely wrong, but I couldn't be mad at him for a long time. I knew that he loved me and did it because he really wanted to know me past my walls. It was inexcusable, but I decided I would forgive him. However, not before I gave him a little bit of trouble first.

"Collin, please stand up. I don't like seeing you this way." It was true. Collin was never one to fall on someone's knees. I didn't like to see him vulnerable.

Collin looked up at me then stood up. I stood up from my seat and walked out of his office wordlessly. I could feel his footsteps behind me as I walked in to the kitchen. I had a smirk on my face as I sat down and continued eating my food. Collin sat down opposite of me, but he wasn't eating.

"Aren't you going to eat?" I asked him calmly.

Collin looked at me with a sad expression. He looked like a little boy whose gift had been taken away from him. "I don't want to eat."

I wanted to wrap my arms around him and tell him that I was not mad at him, but I knew I shouldn't. If he thinks I forgave him easily, he might think that he could get away with anything easily.

"Suit yourself." I shrugged noncommittally as I continued eating.

Once I finished, I held my plate and Collin's plate as well and placed them in the sink. I washed the dishes with soap then rinsed them off with water before drying them and putting them away in the cupboard. I turned around to walk to the living room, and gasped as I saw Collin standing behind me.

"Are you going to stay mad at me, Es?" He asked me. "I already said I'm sorry." I didn't reply and just walked around him, the smirk still plastered on my face. "What would it take for you to forgive me?"

I turned around and looked at him for a moment before I shrugged. "I don't know yet." My answer was noncommittal and with disinterest.

I turned back around and walked to the living room. I sat down on the couch and grabbed the book I was reading from the coffee table and started reading. Collin sat down beside me on the couch and pulled my legs up to his lap then started massaging my feet. It was so relaxing that I couldn't complain, and if Collin thought he was getting extra points then quite honestly he thought right. His hands moved up slowly until it was resting on my thigh. He squeezed it getting my attention. I put my book down and looked at him with a raised eyebrow. He looked at me guiltily and his hands went back to my feet as he massaged them.

"Keep doing that and I might forgive you."

Collin looked up at me and searched my face. "You have already forgiven me, haven't you?"A small smile made its way to my face as I nodded. "You little..." He trailed off as he started tickling me.

"Co... Collin." I managed to squeeze out through my laughs. He stopped tickling me and looked at me. I tried to catch my breath before I spoke. "It doesn't mean that what you did is okay. I understand that you want to know everything about me, but you have to respect that there are some things that I don't want to talk about."

Collin nodded. "I know that now, and I'm sorry. I really am." I nodded and wrapped my arms around his torso and snuggled against his chest. "I mean what I said earlier, Es." Collin's voice vibrated through his chest. "I am willing to pay all of the expenses for Rosa's treatment."

"You don't have to." I told him. "Dad's paying the expenses now."

Collin backed away a little so I pulled back and looked up at him. "Why are you still working then?"

"I can't take the risk of dad leaving again. He did it once, he'll do it again." Collin probably noticed that I wasn't going to back down so he didn't say anything. "I'm tired. Let's go to sleep, babe" I held his hand and stood up then we both walked to the bedroom.

**********Remember to vote, comment, share, recommend, add 'Trixie' to your reading list, and follow. :)

Chapter 24 - That Fateful Night

'Are you out, babe?' I sent Collin a text message.

He replied in no time. 'I'll be there shortly.'

I locked my phone and placed it inside my bag as I made my way out of the strip club. Joe saw me on the way out and gave me a friendly smile.

"Do you want me to hail you a taxi?"

I shook my head with a small smile. "No, thank you. My boyfriend should be here now." He nodded.

"Joe, come here for a second." One of the bodyguards called. Joe looked at me then back at the other bodyguard.

"Go." I waved my hand. "He should be here any minute now." Joe nodded hesitantly before going to speak to the other bodyguard.

I opened my purse to bring out my phone and call Collin to see where he was when I suddenly felt my arm being pulled back, out of its socket, and a hand clamped over my mouth. I was taken into a dark alley then pushed roughly against the walls. I felt the air leave my lungs as my eyes started to water.

"Is it money you want? I'll give you..." I trailed off when I noticed that my purse wasn't with me. I must have dropped it on the floor without even noticing.

The stranger looked at me with a menacing look in his eyes. "Oh no, darling, I want something else." I could tell that he was drunk by the way he slurred on his words.

My heartbeat went haywire as it started pounding hard and fast. I felt as though it was going to beat out of my chest.

"I want something sweeter, darling." His hand suddenly loosened on my mouth, and I screamed.

"Help!"

"Fucking bitch!" He slapped me across my face. It sounded like the crack of a whip, and my head jerked to the side under the force of his hand. "Stay quiet, bitch." He spat as his hand went to my dress and he started lifting it up. My hand went down to my dress trying to pull it back down. "Do not move, you slut, if you cooperate I will make this painless." He removed my hand and grabbed my panties pulling it down. I clamped my thighs together; trying to stall what I knew was going to happen. He held me against the wall with one hand on my throat; choking me, as his other hand started to unzip his pants. By that time, I was in tears. I knew I couldn't do anything to stop him because even though he was drunk, he was till stronger than me. From what I could see through the darkness, he was well built.

I squeezed my eyes shut, wanting to get this over with; the tears still rolling down my face. I waited, but it never came. When I opened my eyes, I saw Collin punching the drunken man relentlessly. I shakily pulled my pants back up and broke out crying. Collin must have heard me cry because he stopped punching the man and looked up at me. He stood up and walked towards me; holding my face in his hands. He didn't say anything and just pulled me into a tight hug. My arms, however, didn't go around him. I was still in shock over what had just happened. My gaze went to the man that was on the floor with blood oozing out of his mouth and nose. I didn't feel sorry for him; I couldn't feel sorry for him. Collin pulled back and held my hand.

"Come one, baby, let me take you home."

I didn't say anything nor reacted in any way as he started walking us to his car. I saw my purse on the ground with all of its contents on the floor.

"My bag" I pointed to the floor. Collin bent down and hastily put everything inside then held it in his hand.

We saw Joe as we were about to step inside his car and he must have probably noticed my disheveled look because he walked towards me with a worried look on his face.

"Trixie? Is everything okay?"

"No, everything is not okay!" Collin yelled. "You are a bodyguard. Your job is to guard the women inside this club which you failed to do. I will make sure that you won't have a job left."

Joe ignored Collin and looked at me. "What happened, Trixie?"

"She was sexually assaulted." I could feel that Collin was trying to control his anger. "Get in the car." He ordered as he looked at me.

Joe looked at me with a guilty expression. "I am sorry." He apologized as I opened the door and stepped inside the car.

I knew Joe had nothing to do with it. I was the one who told him I was fine and he could go talk to the other bodyguard. He shouldn't have felt guilty.

Collin looked sideways at me once we were inside the car, but didn't ask anything. The drive back home was silent. Once we arrived at his penthouse building, he parked the car and stepped out then came around to my side and opened my door. He pulled me out gently and walked us to the elevators. Collin wrapped his arms around me protectively and I relished in the warmth and safety of his embrace. I was more than thankful that he was still not asking me for details since I felt like I couldn't speak. The elevator dinged and the doors opened, we stepped out and Collin unlocked the door to his penthouse. He placed his keys on a nearby table and placed his hands on either side of my arms.

"Es, baby, please tell me you're okay. You haven't uttered a single word yet."

"I'm okay." I said my voice above a whisper. I was far from okay though and it was obvious that Collin could see past my lie.

"Let me run you a bath." He said and walked us to the bedroom.

I stood in the middle of the bathroom with my hands raised as Collin removed my dress then underwear before he undressed as well then turned on the water.

"How is the water?" He asked me gently.

"Okay." My voice was above a whisper.

Collin nodded and held me tight against his body for a moment before he pulled back and grabbed the body wash and poured a little over the sponge and started rubbing it over my body.

"Do you want to talk about it, baby?" He asked quietly. I could feel that he was unsure of how to approach the situation.

I was quiet for a moment before I started speaking. "I was outside the strip club waiting for you, and Joe was with me too, but then someone called him and I told him to go." My voice was shaking. "Suddenly I felt someone grab my arm and push me into the alleyway and against the wall." I continued. "I screamed and he slapped me across my face." Before I could continue, Collin grabbed my face in his hands, and started inspecting it. He muttered some incoherent words under his breath before he placed a soft and gentle kiss where it hurt.

"What happened next?" I could hear the pain in his tone.

"He pulled my dress up and my panties down, and had started to unzip his pants when you came."

"So he didn't...?" He trailed off. I knew what he wanted to ask.

I shook my head. "No, you came before anything could happen."

Collin sighed in relief and pulled me into his arms. He then turned off the water and grabbed a white fluffy towel from the rack and wrapped it around my body before grabbing one for himself as well and wrapping it around his waist. He walked me to the bedroom and I sat down on the bed. I watched as Collin opened the dresser and brought out a pair of my underwear and one of my nightgowns then walked back towards me.

"Do you want me to help you, baby?" He asked me and I shook my head.

He handed me the clothes and I accepted them with a small smile before I removed the towel from around my body and started dressing. Collin grabbed a pair of jogging pants and put them on, then grabbed a t-shirt from the closet and put that on as well.

When we were both dressed, he sat down beside me on the bed and his arm went around my shoulder, pulling me closer to him. "I want to ask you something, Es."

I nodded against his chest, but figured he couldn't see me. "Okay."

"When I found you...you weren't fighting him." I was silent for a moment. I knew what it looked liked from a distance, two consenting adults, when it was far from it. "Es?" He called my name.

I pulled back and looked down as I played with the hem of my nightgown. "I tried, but he was stronger than me." I said in a low voice. "I just gave in to my fate." I said in a whisper.

Collin pulled me in a comforting hug as he smoothed down my hair. My arms instinctively went around him, holding him tight, afraid to let go.

"I am so sorry for what you had to go through, beautiful."

"Don't be sorry, Collin. If it wasn't for you, god knows what would have happened."

He pulled back and tucked a stray hair behind my ear as he looked straight into my eyes. "Baby, get some rest now. Tomorrow we need to talk."

"What do you want to talk about?" I asked him in a low voice.

"Don't worry about it, baby, we can talk tomorrow."

"Collin, please just tell me." I held both of his hands in mine.

Collin looked at me and I could notice his hesitance before he spoke. "I didn't like it that you work as a stripper, but I tried to be okay with it, but after this..." He trailed off.

"What are you saying, Collin?" I asked him with a confused and questioning look on my face.

"I am willing to pay for Rosa's treatment and everything else you ask of me, but no more stripping."

"But..." I tried to reason with him.

"No buts, Es. This time I won't have it. It's either me or stripping."

I looked at him incredulously. "You can't do that. You can't give me an ultimatum."

"I already did, Es. So, what's it going to be?"

"I don't know."

"It shouldn't be that hard." He was furious.

"I don't know, Collin. I don't know." I yelled on the verge of tears.

"Then I think it's best if we take some time apart until you get your priorities straight." I watched as Collin stood up and walked out of the room.

I stayed rooted in my spot unable to understand what had just happened. He left me when I needed his love the most. I wiped the tears with the back of my hands and looked back at the clock beside the bed; a couple more hours until the sun comes up. I stood up from the bed and opened the closet. I grabbed my suitcase from the bottom of the closet and placed it on the bed. I unzipped it then grabbed my clothes from the closet and threw them inside. Zipping the suitcase back up, I sat down on the bed and waited for the sun to come up before I left with my tears still flowing freely down my face.

**********Remember to vote, comment, share, recommend, add 'Trixie' to your reading list, and follow. :)

Chapter 25 - Collin's POV

I walked in to the penthouse feeling exhausted from work. I loosened the tie around my neck and placed my work suitcase on a nearby coffee table then walked in to the kitchen. I opened the fridge, and found some leftover chicken pot pie so I decided to heat it up. Pressing the button on the microwave, I left it to heat up while I went to my room. It was empty and no sign of Esmeralda. I opened the closet and noticed that all of her clothes were gone. Next, I opened the dresser, but everything she owned was gone as well.

I sighed and sat down at the edge of the bed as I rubbed my eyes with the palm of my hands. What did I expect? I was the one who suggested that we take some time apart. It shouldn't have been a shock that she was going to move out. I couldn't help but wonder where she was staying at. Did she go back home even though she wasn't on good terms with her dad, or was she staying at that motel that I picked her up from. I felt myself getting angry at the thought of her staying at such a place. I brought my phone out of my pocket and called her. It rang several times, but she didn't answer so I decided to send her a text.

'Where are you staying at, Es?'

I waited a few minutes for a reply, but it didn't come.

'Es, just tell me if you're okay.'

I hoped she would reply to this one, but still no luck. I was furious with myself. I shouldn't have said what I said to her. I shouldn't have given her an ultimatum, but I hated what she did for a living, god damn it. The way men looked at her body and devoured her with their eyes. The way men grew tents in their pants just by looking at my woman. I growled lowly and stood up from the bed then walked to the kitchen. I grabbed the plate from the microwave and placed it back in the fridge; I had no appetite left.

I made my way to the living room and walked over to the tray that held several alcoholic drinks. I grabbed the bottle of Jack Daniels and a glass cup then sat down on the sofa, poured myself a double shot and took a slug. I grimaced as I poured myself another double shot. As I was about to slug it straight back, the doorbell rang. I groaned and decided to ignore it. I was in no mood to talk to anyone. Unfortunately, the person behind the door was relentless as they took turns in knocking and ringing the bell. I groaned once more before I stood up from my seat and opened the door.

"What do you want?" I asked my brother annoyingly as I kept the door open and walked back to the living room. I heard the door close shut, and Benjamin's footsteps behind me.

"Well, hello to you too, brother." The sarcastic tone was easily detectable.

I decided to ignore him and sat down on the seat I had vacated earlier. I grabbed my shot glass and took a swig.

"Whoa there, brother" Benjamin commented. "If you want to drink, go ahead, but at least offer me a glass."

I shook my head at my brother. "Get one yourself, you're not a stranger." I retorted.

Benjamin tsked sarcastically as he stood up and grabbed a cup. I watched him as he sat back down and poured a single shot. He downed the drink and grimaced before looking around the penthouse as if searching for someone.

"Where is Esmeralda?" He asked me.

"She's gone."

"What do you mean gone?" He asked with a questioning look on his face.

"We broke up and she left."

"What? Why? Weren't you head over heels in love with her? What gives?"

"Leave me alone, Ben." I muttered sounding irritated.

"No, tell me what's wrong." He was unrelenting.

"We had a fight and we broke up." I told him exasperated as I poured myself another shot.

"Yes, but why?"

I downed the drink in my hand before I spoke. "I went yesterday to pick her up from the strip club and found a man forcing himself on her."

"What?" Benjamin yelled, and I could feel him getting furious. "What was she doing at the strip club anyways?"

"Oh, yea, she's a stripper." I raised my glass up before downing it all in one swig.

"Esmeralda is a stripper?" Benjamin questioned himself in a low voice.

"Yup" I agreed. I could feel myself getting dizzy.

"I still don't understand why you broke up."

"I asked her to choose either me or her job, but she couldn't choose. I told her we should take some time apart until she got her priorities in order."

"She gets assaulted and that's how you help her?" Benjamin asked incredulously. "You are a fool!"

I definitely didn't need him to tell me what I already knew, what I already was berating myself over. "Don't tell me what I already know, Ben. I already hate myself for what I did. I can't believe I let her go." I didn't know if it was the alcohol reacting in my body, but I felt tears gathering on the corner of my eyes.

"Then get her back."

"No." I shook my head as I poured another glass, but I couldn't drink it since Benjamin took it forcibly away from me.

"What do you mean no?" He asked me infuriately.

"I am not going to take her back as long as she's a stripper. If she wants me, she has to quit."

"Stripping is a profession just like any other profession."

"You say that because you don't see the looks she gets whenever she's on stage."

"Of course she gets looks; she is a very beautiful lady." I tried to hold in my anger as I looked at Benjamin. "What? You're mad because I'm saying the truth?" He taunted. "Esmeralda is a very beautiful lady, and she would get looks no matter what job she worked."

"Yes, but it won't be the same." I argued.

"Whatever, you're an idiot and I am more than sure that you know it."

I ignored his comment then said. "She's not on good terms with her father so I don't know if she went back home or is living in some motel. Can you make sure? She's not answering my calls."

"Do you want me to go to her place?"

"Yes." I slurred and gave him her address.

"Okay, but it's getting late now so I won't go until tomorrow."

"What if she needs some place to sleep?" I was getting worried over her.

"Esmeralda is a big girl. She knows how to handle herself." Benjamin assured me. "Do you mind if I crash here tonight?"

"Whatever" I muttered.

I knew Benjamin wanted to crash at my place because he didn't want to leave me alone when I was that drunk, and to be honest I was thankful. I didn't want to do something stupid like go over to

Esmeralda's house. I sighed and stood up from my seat. I needed to take a shower and change my clothes because I reeked of alcohol.

"Where are you going?" Benjamin asked me as he saw me stand up.

"I need to take a shower then go to bed."

"Aren't you going to have dinner? I'm starving." He rubbed his stomach.

I shook my head no. "Help yourself to anything. I'm not hungry." I turned around and started to walk away.

As soon as I walked in to the bedroom, I froze. It hit me like a ton of bricks, Esmeralda was gone. I could no longer wake up to her every morning. I could no longer kiss her, touch her, and feel her. I lost her. I couldn't stay in the room; it reminded me so much of her, and I didn't want to be reminded of her. I grabbed the stuff I needed and walked out. I went to one of the spare rooms and took my bath in the en suite bathroom. I felt my stomach grumble as I walked out so I put on a clean t-shirt and trousers and walked out to the kitchen.

"I knew you would change your mind." Benjamin said as he saw me walk inside the kitchen then placed a plate of recently heated chicken pot pie on the table before putting another plate in the microwave. I sat down on the table and started eating, Benjamin followed a few minutes later.

"I miss her." I admitted as I pushed my food around the plate.

"You know what you have to do."

Benjamin said as he placed a spoonful of the chicken pot pie in his mouth.

"It's easy for you to say."

"It's easy if you want it to be. Esmeralda didn't do anything wrong. If she chose to be a stripper then you should respect her decision."

"I tried to."

"Then you should have tried harder." Benjamin retorted as he placed his utensils down and pushed his plate away. "Her profession might not be a noble profession like a doctor's profession is, for instance, but she's a grown woman and she can make her decisions on her own." I placed my head in my hand and squeezed my eyes shut. "You know." Benjamin started with a small chuckle. "I have never seen you this way, not even when you and Sienna broke up."

I opened my eyes and looked at him. "Esmeralda is the one."

Benjamin nodded then stood up from his seat and held his empty plate in his hands. He placed it in the sink then turned around and looked at me. "I'm going to sleep." He informed me and I nodded.

I stood up as well and placed my half eaten plate in the sink then switched off the lights before walking in to the spare bedroom. I felt like something was missing as I lay down on the bed, and that something or rather someone was Esmeralda. I was going to stand by my word though. I didn't want the woman I love to be a stripper, and if she was unable to do that then I was unable to be with her.

**********Remember to vote, comment, share, recommend, add 'Trixie' to your reading list, and follow. :)

Chapter 26 - A New Page

"Mom?" I called out in a hoarse voice as I walked inside the house. "Rosa?" I called my sister, but no one seemed to be at home.

I then remembered that Rosalinda had a doctor's appointment and mom was accompanying her. With my duffel bag around my shoulder, I started walking towards my old bedroom.

"Es?" I heard my dad's voice.

Great! I was hoping I wouldn't bump into him. I turned around and looked at him. He was probably watching T.V in the living room because he was holding the remote control in his hand. His gaze went to my duffel bag before it settled back on me.

"Is everything okay?" He asked, probably because he noticed my red and puffy eyes.

"Everything's fine." I muttered annoyingly as I turned back around and continued walking to my room.

"Is it Collin? Did he hurt you?" I could hear the anger in his voice.

I turned around suddenly feeling protective of Collin for some reason.

"He is more of a man than you'll ever be." I spat out, but instantly regretted what I said once I saw the hurt in my dad's eyes. "I'm..." I started, wanting to apologize when he interrupted me.

"You have every right to say that, Es. I wasn't a good father and I acknowledge that, but I'm trying to be better."

I nodded. I knew he was trying hard to make things work, or at least that was what Rosalinda had been telling me whenever she called.

"Do you have time?" I asked him wanting to talk to someone, and at that moment I didn't care that that someone was my dad.

A sincere and hopeful smile made its way to my dad's face. "Of course, I have all the time in the world for my baby girl." I smiled and dropped my duffel bag to the ground then walked with my dad to the living room.

"Collin broke up with me." I started as we sat down on the couch. Dad nodded for me to continue. "I love him." I started bawling my eyes out. I wasn't going to delve into details.

Dad wrapped his arms around my shoulders and started saying soothing words in my ears trying to calm me down. Once he felt me calm down a bit, he pulled back from the hug and looked at me.

"If it is meant to be, he'll come back and if not then at least you experienced something nice with him." He offered his piece of wisdom.

I nodded sadly. "Thank you, dad, I really needed that." I told him honestly. "A little breakdown does wonders for a girl." I chuckled and my dad joined in as well.

"Es, I know it's probably not a good time, but I need to talk to you."

I sniffed. "Sure."

"Your mom has told me how you have been working late hours at night until the early hours of the morning to help with Rosalinda's treatment expenses." I noticed the guilty expression on his face, but nodded nonetheless. "I know that maybe I don't have a say in it." He said sadly. "But I want you to quit. Find a nine-to-five job, even if it doesn't pay as much. I'm going to pay all of the expenses and not just for Rosalinda's treatment." I could see the sincerity in his eyes. "I made the biggest mistake when I left before, but I promise you it won't happen again." I knew that my dad was telling the truth. His eyes spoke before his words.

I nodded with a smile on my face. "I forgive you, dad." I suddenly said.

I could tell that he was shocked for a moment from the way his eyes widened before a smile broke onto his face.

"I am so happy to hear that coming from you, baby girl. I am so sorry for what I put you, your mother, and your sister through."

"Stop apologizing, dad. What's done is done. From now on we open a fresh new page with new memories." Dad nodded with a smile and hugged me tight.

A few moments later, I stood up from my seat and walked to my bedroom. I washed my face to freshen up then applied a little bit of makeup to hide the fact that I was crying before I grabbed my bag and headed to the strip club.

"Come in."

Conner looked at me, a look of surprise etched on his face. "Trixie? I didn't know you were working the morning schedule."

"I'm not." I told him. "I'm actually here to quit."

Conner looked at me with a questioning look on his face. "Take a seat. Let's talk about this." I sat down on the chair in front of his desk. "Why do you want to quit? Is it because of your boyfriend?"

I wasn't quitting because of Collin. I was quitting because I knew that my dad wouldn't leave, and that we were financially stable. I wanted to lead a normal life and have a normal job where I wouldn't be ashamed to talk about.

"I'm looking for a normal job."

"Well, this is a normal job." He said trying to stifle a laugh.

"Yeah, it's very normal to strip down to your birthday suit for strangers to ogle." I chuckled.

Conner nodded. "Touché" He chuckled. "It's a shame though. You are one of my best dancers. You bring the customers in."

I shrugged and stood up. "Anyways I have to get going." Conner stood up as well and I watched as he came around to my side. "Even though we bickered all the time, you are a good manager and dare I say friend." Conner lips turned upwards in a smile as he pulled me into a hug. I wrapped my arms around him and hugged him as well.

#

"Rosa." I called my sister's name giving her a heads up before I opened the door. I saw her rushing to her vanity mirror to put on her wig. "Rosa, sweetie, you don't need to put the wig around me."

She stopped in her tracks, but didn't turn around to look at me. "I don't like people seeing me bald." She said with a shrug.

"I'm not anyone, Rosa." I told her as I walked towards her. "And it's just hair it will grow out eventually. You look beautiful either way."

Rosalinda hesitantly turned around and looked up at me through her lashes. "You don't think I look weird?" She asked me.

"Weird? Ha." I chuckled and flopped down on her bed. "You are the most beautiful girl, sweetie." I saw a smile make its way to her face and I patted the bed. She flopped down beside me as we both looked at the ceiling. "How was your chemotherapy session today?"

"As usual; long and exhausting"

I turned my head sideways and looked at her. "I'm sorry I couldn't be there."

Rosalinda gave me a sincere smile. "It's okay." She looked back up at the ceiling. "So you and Collin broke up?"

"Mm..." I made a sound of agreement as I looked up the ceiling as well.

"I really liked him."

"Yeah, I liked him too." I conceded.

"What happened?" She asked me.

I couldn't tell her the details of the breakup because that would include me telling her about the stripping and the almost rape. No one knew about both of those stories, and I wanted to keep it that way.

"We just had a disagreement about something." My sister noticed that I didn't want to give any information so she stopped asking.

"You're okay with dad now?" She asked me.

A small smile appeared on my face as I answered. "Yeah"

"What happened that made you forgive him?"

"When I came home, you and mom weren't around and I needed to talk to someone. He gave me the fatherly advice that I was used to and I kind of missed that." I informed her.

"He's trying really hard. He really regrets what he had done."

"I know." I told her honestly. "I really miss this." I told her as I looked sideways at her. "We haven't sat and talked like this in a very long time."

"Yeah" Rosalinda said sadly still looking up the ceiling.

Just then my phone vibrated inside my pocket. I pulled my phone out and Collin's name lighted the screen.

"Collin?" Rosalinda asked me as her eyes went to my phone's screen.

"Yes." I sighed as I waited for him to end the call before I placed it on the bed beside me.

A few seconds after my phone stopped vibrating, I received a new text message.

'Where are you staying at, Es?'

A few minutes later another one arrived.

'Es, just tell me if you're okay.'

I didn't reply to either one of the messages. He was the one that decided to leave me. I had to admit that it hadn't been twenty four hours yet and I had missed him. I wondered if he had eaten dinner or not. I knew he would be exhausted from work. I groaned and shrugged off my thoughts. If I kept thinking about him, I would start crying all over again and I didn't want to do that. My eyes were already red and puffy enough.

"Do we have any ice cream left in the freezer?" I asked Rosalinda sadly.

Rosalinda chuckled and stood up. "I don't know, let's see."

I stood up and watched her as she put her wig on before we walked out to the kitchen. We found half a tub of Vanilla Swiss Almond in the freezer. I grabbed two spoons and both Rosalinda and I dug in. We spent the rest of the night talking and stuffing our face with ice cream before we retired to bed.

#

I woke up the next morning to the doorbell ringing. I groaned and stood up from the bed knowing that no one was home to answer the door. I slipped on my fuzzy slippers and walked out of my room. The doorbell rang again. I internally cursed whoever was at the door before I opened it. I was surprised to see who was at the door.

"Ben?" Surprise laced my tone.

"We need to talk."

**********Remember to vote, comment, share, recommend, add 'Trixie' to your reading list, and follow. :)

Chapter 27 - Plan Gone Wrong

I hooked my arm through Benjamin's as we walked inside the Edward's residence. The party was in full swing. Waiters were going around with trays of canapés and cocktails. Everyone was in their expensive suit and tie, and sipping on their champagne.

"Do I look okay?" I whispered in Benjamin's ear suddenly feeling self conscious.

Benjamin looked at me sideways. "You look more than okay. You're the prettiest woman in this room." Color rose to my cheek as I murmured thanks. Benjamin chuckled and planted a kiss on my cheek.

"Let's go see where mom and dad are." I nodded and we started walking out to the garden.

There were even more people out than there were inside. However, it wasn't hard to spot Mr. and Mrs. Edwards. We walked towards them and I could see a smile forming on both of their faces as they saw us coming.

"Esmeralda." Margaret gave me a smile and pulled me into a hug. "How are you, sweetheart?" She asked me once she pulled back.

"I'm good." I answered shyly. "Happy anniversary"

"Thank you, sweetheart. I'm happy you came. Collin told me that you weren't coming." she told me.

I didn't know what to say so I couldn't be more thankful when Benjamin answered for me. "I managed to change her mind." I turned sideways and gave him a smile. "Is Collin here?" Benjamin asked. "Did he arrive or not yet?"

"He arrived about half an hour ago." Silas responded and Benjamin nodded.

"Okay, we have to go and mingle. Try to have some fun, but not too much fun." Margaret laughed before her and Silas walked away.

I looked around the garden, and my eyes caught Collin with Sienna holding onto his arm like he was her security blanket. Collin must have noticed eyes on him because he looked up, and his eyes met mine.

"You're way more beautiful than her." Benjamin whispered in my ear.

A smile made its way to my face and then suddenly I felt him planting a kiss on my cheek. I turned sideways to face him and wrapped my arms around his neck.

"He's walking towards us." He whispered in my ear and I felt the palm of my hands starting to sweat and my heart beating fast. "Relax." He soothed.

"Esmeralda, Ben."

I released my arms from around Benjamin's neck and turned to look at Collin who had a thunderous look on his face.

"Collin." Benjamin nodded, but I didn't reply.

I was too busy looking at his handsome face. God, how I longed to run my fingers through his hair, wrap my arms around his neck and kiss those luscious lips of his. Stop it, Es. My mind berated me.

"What are you doing with her?" He asked his brother with anger lacing his tone.

"What does it look like I'm doing?" Benjamin retorted in a very cool tone.

"I am not in the mood to play your games, Ben." Collin clenched his jaw and I could see him clenching his fists at his side as if struggling for control.

"We're dating." He snaked his arm around my waist and pulled me closer to his side. "You had your chance with her and you lost it. "

Collin looked at my face as if searching for some sort of confirmation. If he was a cartoon character, steam would be coming out of his ears, and before I could blink, Collin swung his hand back and punched Benjamin in the face. I gasped and looked at Benjamin who didn't fight back. He just looked at Collin with a smirk on his face as he wiped the blood off of his mouth.

"Aren't you going to fight back, brother?" Collin taunted, but Benjamin stayed put.

"What is going on here?" Silas's voice thundered.

I looked up and just then noticed the crowd that had gathered around us. Margaret had rushed to her injured son while Silas looked furious as he waited for someone to answer him, but no one did. Instead, I felt Collin roughly grab my hand and drag me out.

Earlier that week

"We need to talk." Benjamin announced as he stood at my doorstep.

"Is everything okay?" I asked him worriedly. "Is Collin okay?" Benjamin nodded wordlessly. I sighed in relief before I stepped back and let him inside.

"Nice home" He commented as he looked around the modest living room.

"Thank you." I gave him a small smile.

"Would you like some coffee?"

"Yes, please." He grinned.

I nodded and walked to the kitchen. I started the coffee machine then brought out two mugs from the cupboard. As I waited for the coffee machine to finish, I wondered why Benjamin was at my place. He had never been here before. Before I could think about it any further, the coffee machine beeped indicating it had finished. I poured the coffee into the two mugs then walked back out to the living room. I handed Benjamin his coffee before sitting on the couch beside him.

"You're probably wondering why I'm here." Benjamin started. I nodded as my hold on the mug tightened. "Collin told me that he broke up with you so he wanted me to check on you. He wanted to know where you're staying and if you're okay." I was about to answer when he stopped me. "I'm here for something else though."

I looked at him questioningly. "What are you here for?" I asked him hesitantly.

"Collin loves you. He is smitten by you." I had a small smile on my face as I heard him say that. "However, he is one stubborn man, and he won't get back with you unless you quit stripping."

My face suddenly turned bright red. Part of it was because I was embarrassed that Benjamin knew that I was a stripper and the other part was because I was mad at Collin for telling him that.

"You know about my job?"

Benjamin nodded. "Let's just say Collin was drunk as a lord last night and blurted out some things that he probably shouldn't have."

"What... what else did he say?" I asked hesitantly.

Benjamin was hesitant for a moment before he said. "He might have told me about the man that sexually assaulted you." His voice was sad.

"Oh my god" I gasped and turned my face sideways, horrified that Collin had told him that.

"Es" Benjamin scooted closer towards me. "It's okay. I don't judge you for being a stripper nor do I judge you for what that... that bastard did to you." I turned my face to look at him and I noticed that he was angry. "It is not your fault, Es."

I nodded hesitantly. "I still don't understand what you need from me."

Collin's lips turned upward in a smile, all of his anger suddenly gone. "Collin thinks you're the one and I have to agree." It was my turn to smile. "So we have to get you two back together."

I nodded. "I love him more than words could say, but he left me when I needed him the most. He left me when I needed his support and love."

"He knows that and he regrets it, but like I said he is too stubborn to take you back unless you leave your job."

"I already quit yesterday." I told him in a low voice.

"You did?" He asked elatedly. "Oh, that's great. When I tell him he would come here instantly."

I shook my head. "I could've called him yesterday and told him, but I didn't."

"Yes, why didn't you?" he asked me confused.

"Like I said, he left me when I needed him the most. He needs to know that that is not acceptable. If I give in this easily to him, he would do it every single time. I have already felt abandoned once; I don't need to experience it again."

"Okay." Benjamin dragged out as he appeared to be thinking. "You do want him back though, don't you?"

I nodded as a small smile made its way to my face. "More than anything"

Benjamin nodded. "Here's the plan." I leaned forward and listened closely as he explained to me how his parents were having an anniversary party in their home the following week. The plan was to go to the party together and act as lovebirds. We both knew that that would make Collin go crazy and make him not want to hurt me again.

Benjamin and I kept in touch every day. He kept me updated with everything regarding Collin which was something I appreciated. He even went shopping with me to buy the dress that I would wear to the anniversary party. He was really a sweetheart.

Back to the anniversary night

"You're hurting me, Collin." I pulled my hand out of his hold.

"What are you doing with my brother?" He demanded in a thunderous voice.

"It's none of your business. You left me, remember?" I raised my chin defiantly.

"You are off limits to other men." His voice was low and threatening. I didn't reply and just turned around to walk back inside and check on Benjamin.

"Don't you dare to go back inside." He threatened.

I turned around and looked at him through narrowed eyes. "You hit your brother." I stated the obvious. "If you don't care about him then it's up to you, but I do. I'm going to check on him." I turned back around and started to walk inside when he stopped me again.

"I will leave without you."

"I came without you, I could leave without you." I told him without turning around then made my way inside.

I found Silas and Margaret talking amongst their guests, but no sign of Benjamin. I walked over to them and they both turned to look at me. Luckily they didn't have grim looks on their faces considering the fight was because of me. Instead they were smiling.

"Do you know where Benjamin is?" I asked them timidly.

"He's in my office." Silas informed.

"Let me take you to him, sweetheart." I nodded thankfully as Margaret led me to Silas's office. I was glad that she didn't ask me questions. She opened the door and let men in then walked back out to mingle with the guests.

I found Benjamin nursing his chin with an ice packet. He looked up at me once he heard my footsteps.

"Are you okay?" I asked him as I sat down beside him on the large brown couch.

"I've been better." He chuckled. "Why are you still here?" He asked me confused. "I thought you would have left with Collin by now."

I shook my head. "I couldn't leave knowing that you were hurt."

"You should've left. Now you ruined the plan." He whined.

I chuckled. "No, Collin ruined the plan when he hit you. He was only supposed to get mad, not hit you." Benjamin just shrugged. "Here let me see that."

I scooted closer to him and grabbed the ice packet from his hand. The wound seemed to have been cleaned up quite nicely.

"Mom cleaned it up for me." He informed me. "She's used to this since she raised two very crazy boys."

"You got that right." I chuckled as Benjamin took the ice packet back from me and placed it back on his chin.

"Go out to him." He waved me off.

"He probably already went home. He said he was leaving without me." I said sadly.

"Well, that needs to be fixed."

Benjamin said as he stood up from his seat. He threw the ice packet in the dustbin and looked at me. "Come on, let's go. I'm taking you to his place."

Benjamin drove me to Collin's penthouse and I could feel my heart beating out of my chest. I was anxious, afraid of what would happen between us.

"It will be okay." Benjamin assured me, noticing my anxiousness. "Collin loves you." I nodded.

A few minutes later, Benjamin stopped his car in front of Collin's building. I took a big breath before I opened the door and stepped out.

"Good luck, Es!" Benjamin gave me thumbs up. I smiled nervously before walking inside the building.

**********Remember to vote, comment, share, recommend, add 'Trixie' to your reading list, and follow. :)

Chapter 28 - "You're the only one that owns my heart."

I greeted the concierge before making my way to the elevator. Luckily, he didn't need to call Collin and inform him of my arrival since he knew me from when I used to live there.

I put in the code to Collin's penthouse, and patted my foot as I waited for the elevator to reach the designated floor.

Needless to say, I was a bundle of nerves.

The elevator dinged, announcing its arrival, and the door opened. I was like a cat on bricks as I raised my hand and rang the doorbell. I waited a few seconds, but Collin didn't open the door. I rang the doorbell again, and this time Collin opened the door. He was still wearing the clothes I saw him in from his parents' anniversary party. We looked at each other for a second before he broke the silence.

"What do you want?" There was so much hatred and anger in his voice.

"I was hoping we could talk." My voice was weak as I wrung my hands nervously.

"I have nothing to say to you."

I ignored the hostility in his tone as I gathered up the courage and said firmly . "Then you will listen to what I have to say." Collin stood aside letting me in.

I felt sick with apprehension as I sat on the couch opposite of Collin. He was looking at me with so much hatred in his eyes, and to be honest, I didn't blame him.

"You wanted to talk, so talk."

I nodded. "Your brother and I, it's not what you think."

Collin looked at me with a raised eyebrow. "I think we already established that fact that you're dating him." He said with so much disgust and repulsion in his tone.

"We're not dating." My voice was above a whisper.

"Oh, you're not?" He mocked. "Then I should get my eyes tested." I looked up at him. "You had your arms around him. He was kissing your cheek while you giggled."

"Yes, but...."

"But, what Esmeralda?" He roared.

"It was all an act."

"An act?" He looked at me, confusion written all over his face.

"Yes, an act." I said. "Benjamin visited me at home about a week ago. He wanted to get us back together, but as much as I wanted to, I wanted you to feel the pain and abandonment I felt when you left me at my weakest moment." Collin looked away guilty. "Benjamin and I came up with a plan. I wanted to make you jealous. I wanted to make you feel the way I felt when you left me." Collin had a mixture of emotions on his face that I couldn't figure out. "I know it was wrong to do something like that, and I'm sorry."

Collin stood up from his seat and sat down beside me. "So you're not dating my brother?" He asked me wanting further confirmation.

I shook my head no. "Benjamin is a wonderful guy, but you're the only one that owns my heart."

Collin's lips turned upwards in a smile, and I couldn't help but smile back.

However, the smile was gone as soon as it came. "I still can't be with you though. I can't sleep at night knowing you're at the strip club where men are ogling you." He shook his head. "I can't."

The smile didn't leave my face. "You don't have to."

"What do you mean?" He had a questioning look on his face.

"I quit." Collin's eyes widened. "I quit stripping."

"Are you serious right now or is this some kind of joke?" he asked warily.

"Very serious" I nodded my head with a smile.

Collin wrapped his arms around my waist, hugging me. "You don't know how much I love you, Es."

I pulled back from the hug and looked at him. "You and Sienna..." I started hesitantly. "Did you get back with each other?" I asked him even though I was afraid of what the answer would be.

Collin shook his head no. "She saw me at the party alone so she figured out that we had broken up. She was trying to get me back telling me how much she misses me, but I wasn't having it." I nodded "You're the only one that owns my heart." He borrowed my line from earlier.

"Kiss me." I told him breathless.

Collin didn't need to be told twice. He crashed his lips to mine and ravished my lips hungrily. I tugged on his shirt wanting more. He pulled back from the kiss and started unbuttoning his shirt. I placed soft kisses on his chest as he unbuttoned his shirt.

"You're killing me, Es." He groaned and reclaimed my lips as I removed his unbuttoned shirt.

"Collin, bedroom" I said breathlessly.

Collin nodded and held me bridal style then walked us to the bedroom. He placed me down on my feet and turned me around so that my back was to him. He unzipped my dress and it pooled around my feet before he started kissing my bare shoulder sending tingles down my spine then unclasped my bra. His expert hands massaged my breasts making my nipples erect. He then turned me around and placed a soft kiss on my lips.

"Lay down, baby." He ordered.

I walked backwards until my legs hit the bed then lay down on my back. Collin kneeled down between my legs and gently slipped down my panties. His gaze went up to me as his eyes met mine. His eyes were dark with desire. He placed his hand on the inside of my thigh and gently spread them apart then started trailing soft kisses on my inner thighs making me shiver and moan with pleasure. I suddenly felt his lips on my slit sending me high with pleasure before he looked up at me.

"Do you like that, beautiful?" He asked me.

That wicked man. I knew what he was doing. He wanted to hear me say that I loved it. Well, I wasn't going to give him the satisfaction.

"It's okay." I shrugged nonchalantly even though I was burning up with desire inside.

"Then maybe I should stop." He said as he started to move away.

"Just get you face back where it belongs." I told him unable to hold it in anymore. I needed him.

Collin chuckled before his face once again disappeared between my thighs. I pulled on his hair relishing in the sweet sensations that were going through my body.

"Collin, I need you inside me."

"How bad do you want it?" He teased.

I couldn't handle it. I wanted him, no I needed him. I looked at him and bit my lip to prevent myself from begging him. Finally, he stopped and swiftly removed his trousers and boxers before climbing on top of me. He grabbed a condom from inside his bedside table drawer and pulled it over his long, thick shaft. He moved the tip in and out of me, teasing me. He had complete control over me, I was at his mercy.

Damn it! I wanted to scream and beg him to stop torturing me and just enter me already.

'"Collin" I pleaded with my eyes for him to go further.

"Beg me." He smirked. I bit my lip and hesitated. Was he really going to tease me like that? "I'm still waiting." His smirk never left his face as he kept moving the tip in and out of me.

"Please, Collin."

"Please what?"

Oh god, he was going to make me spell it out for him. "Please fuck me." I mumbled.

"What was that you said?" He asked with his trademark smirk plastered on his face. "I didn't hear you."

"Fuck me, Collin. I need you inside me." My voice was loud and clear.

Without a warning, Collin plunged into me. He started with slow thrusts as I moaned. He pulled out and plunged back into me long and hard. My hands raked his back as I closed my eyes and got lost in the sensation. My orgasm started building and our breathing became heavy. I opened my eyes and started kissing Collin's neck before our mouths found each other. Collin pulled back from the kiss and groaned as his strokes became harder and faster.

"Collin." I moaned as I felt my orgasm reaching its peak. Collin took my nipple in his mouth, and that did it for me I called out his name in ecstasy and came apart in a violent shudder. All I could see were the stars in my eyes courtesy of the explosion that rocked my body.

Collin kept slamming his hips into me with powerful thrusts until I felt him still completely and he came inside me.

"Oh god, Es"

He laid his head on my shoulder, both us silent only the sound of our heavy breathing could be heard. My fingers played with his hair as we both tried to catch our breaths.

A few moments later, he pulled out of me, removed the condom, and threw it in the dustbin. He then curled up next to me with his head resting on my breast. He felt so close to me. The heat from his skin was so intense.

"What made you quit stripping?" I heard him ask me.

My fingers ran through his hair unconsciously as I replied. "My dad and I talked the day we broke up. We reconciled and I forgave him. He promised that he won't leave us and he acknowledges that he made a mistake the first time around." I told him. "I believe him."

"So it's not because of me?" The disappointment in Collin's voice didn't go unnoticed.

"It was partly because of you and partly because I didn't really like my job in the first place, but dad assuring me that he wouldn't leave us gave me the assurance I needed."

Collin kissed my bare belly then stood up proudly in all his naked glory. "I'm starving. Feed me woman."

I chuckled. "You've got it all wrong. You're cooking me something to eat." I gave him a cheeky smile. "Would you please give me a t-shirt to put on?"

"Why? I like you naked."

"Collin." I laughed.

He chuckled and walked over to his drawer. He brought out a t-shirt and handed it to me before grabbing jogging pants for himself and putting it on. Putting the t-shirt on, I stood up from the bed and walked out to the kitchen with Collin on my heels.

I sat at the kitchen table and looked at Collin who had his eyebrows raised at me.

"If you cook for me, I'll let you join me later in the shower."

That got him going. He quickly opened the fridge with a smile on his face as he brought out the things he needed.

**********Remember to vote, comment, share, recommend, add 'Trixie' to your reading list, and follow. :)

Chapter 29 - Peacemaker

"I'll get it." I yelled as I walked hurriedly to the front door to open it.

Collin stood there in his casual jeans and top, but still looking sexy as hell.

"Hey, handsome" I leaned forward and placed a chaste kiss on his lips.

"I miss you." He wrapped his arms around my waist.

"I miss you too." I smiled.

"Well, if you move in with me..."

"Es, who's there?" Mom's voice sounded from the other room, interrupting what Collin was about to say.

Even though we made up, I had yet to move back into Collin's penthouse. I wanted to spend more time at home with my parents and sister. Collin however wasn't happy about it; he wanted me all to himself.

"It's Collin, mom." I yelled back. Collin released his hold from around my waist and I took hold of his hand. "Come on, handsome. Let's go inside before they start wondering what we're up to."

Collin smirked. "Well if I had my way we would be up against this wall."

"Good thing you don't." I retorted with a cheeky smile as we walked inside the living room.

My dad stood up from his seat and greeted Collin politely. He looked like he wanted to give him a lecture about dating his daughter, but I knew he wouldn't because he was still wary about anything that concerned me. He didn't want to ruin what we had just reestablished.

Rosalinda looked up at Collin with a huge smile on her face. "Hi." She greeted him with a wave of her hand.

"Hey, Rosa, How are you doing?" He had a huge smile on his face.

"I'm okay." She shrugged.

Just then, my mom appeared at the doorway with a friendly smile on her face. "Collin, how are you?"

"I'm good, Mrs. Roberts." He gave her one of his white Hollywood smiles.

She gave him a smile back. "Lunch is ready." She informed us.

Dad was the first one up as he walked out to the dining room and mom followed after him. Rosalinda stayed back with me and Collin.

"Aren't you going to eat? She asked us.

"We'll be right there, sweetie. I'm just waiting for someone." She nodded then stood up and followed mom and dad to the dining room.

"Who are you waiting for?" Collin asked me.

Before I could reply, the doorbell rang. I jumped up from my seat and opened the door.

"Hey." I greeted him with a hug.

"Is he here?" He asked me and I nodded before I started walking back to the living room.

Collin stood up from his seat as soon as we walked in. The anger on his face was easily detectable.

"What are you doing here?" He asked his brother sharply.

"Ben is here to have lunch with us." I answered on behalf of Benjamin.

"If he's staying then I'm going." He said as he turned his face up defiantly.

Benjamin sighed. "We tried, Es." He said sadly. "I'll just go."

Collin was adamant about not talking to Benjamin even after I told him that it was all an act. His reasoning was that Benjamin was his brother and shouldn't have done what he did. I couldn't sleep at night knowing that both of them were not talking because of me so I decided to invite Benjamin over and end this once and for all.

"No, you won't." I told Benjamin firmly even though my gaze was directed at Collin. "This nonsense will stop now." Collin was still looking up defiantly. "You know very well that this was my fault. Benjamin was just the accomplice." I explained. "You should thank him not be mad at him. If it wasn't for him, you wouldn't have gotten jealous and wanted me back."Collin was still unresponsive. I looked at Benjamin. "Say something, Ben."

Benjamin nodded. "Collin, you know I did this to get you two back together. You have punished me enough with your silent treatment."

Collin looked like a little boy who was mad at his parents for saying no to him.

"Oh, stop it already. I know very well that you miss your brother."

Collin's face softened as he looked at us with a small smile forming on his face the suddenly, he walked forward and pulled his brother into a hug. Benjamin was stunned at first and frozen in place, but then his arms wrapped around his brother as well.

"I'm sorry. I really am." Benjamin apologized as he pulled back.

Collin patted him on his back. "If you do it again, I will personally hunt you down and kill you with my bare hands."

I stifled a laugh at Benjamin's expression as I grabbed Collin's hand. "Do not bully your brother." I scolded him. "Come on, let's eat. Food is getting cold."

"Oh, Ben, you have arrived." My mom greeted him with a smile.

"Hey, Mrs. Roberts, Mr. Roberts" He took a seat beside Rosalinda. "Hey, pretty girl."

"Hey, Ben" She smiled shyly.

Benjamin and I had gotten close through everything that had happened, and I can honestly say that my family liked him as well.

"This is the best chicken casserole I have ever tasted." Benjamin complimented my mom on her cooking. She had made her special chicken and leek casserole with mushroom sauce recipe.

"Kiss ass." Collin coughed, but it was very clear what he had said. I chuckled and nudged his ribs.

"You're just jealous because I complimented her and you didn't." Benjamin said teasingly.

Collin scoffed. "I don't need to compliment her. Mrs. Roberts knows that she makes the best food I have ever tasted."

"Kiss ass." I coughed, borrowing his line, and the whole table fell into fits of laughter.

#

"Who is ready for dessert?" I asked in a sing song voice as I walked in to the living room with a scrumptious looking pecan pie in my hand.

"I do." Benjamin jumped up excitedly. I chuckled and shook my head at that man's antics.

Mom entered behind me with empty plates and utensils in her hand. I grabbed an empty plate from her hand and cut a slice for Benjamin before cutting each one a piece.

"Baby?" Collin whispered in my ear as everyone else was busy conversing.

"Mm..?" I looked up at him.

"Come home with me."

I looked at Collin for a moment before I replied. "We already talked about this, babe."

"Just today" He pleaded. "I miss you."

I stared at him for a moment and saw the need and want in his eyes. "Okay." I agreed.

Collin smiled happily, leaned forward and kissed me. "I love you, beautiful."

"I love you too, handsome."

"Aw, I love you too." We heard Ben say.

I turned to face him with my cheeks painted red with embarrassment. Collin snaked his arm around my waist and pulled me closer to him as I hid my face in his chest.

#

"Baby, should I order takeout pizza?" Collin called out from behind the bathroom door as I took my shower after our love making session.

"Yes, please. I want pepperoni with extra cheese."

After my shower, I grabbed my pajamas from my overnight bag that I had brought with me, and put it on before I walked out to the living room where Collin was. I joined him on the couch and curled up against him.

"What are you watching, babe?"

He turned sideways to look at me with a heartwarming smile on his face.

"Golf" He informed me.

"Old man" I teased.

Collin scoffed. "Do you want a repeat of earlier to show you what this old man can do?" He challenged.

I chuckled. "No, thank you. I am drained out of energy."

Collin smirked at me, and before he could give me some teasing remark, the doorbell rang. He stood up from his seat to open the door then came back a few minutes later with two pizza boxes in his hand.

"This is so good." I said as I placed the delicious piece of pizza in my mouth.Collin didn't reply as he ate the pizza hungrily. We were both drained out of energy form our earlier love making session. We watched TV as we ate while I curled up against him. It felt so good being so close to him. Once we were done, Collin looked at me suggestively.

"What?" I asked him confused.

"Round two?" He asked with a wiggle of his eyebrows.

I chuckled before I started removing his shirt.

**********Remember to vote, comment, share, recommend, add 'Trixie' to your reading list, and follow. :)

Chapter 30 - The Proposal

Dr. David Patel looked at us with a poker face. I couldn't figure out if what he was about to tell us was good news or bad news.

"I am happy to inform you that Rosalinda's body has responded very well to the chemotherapy treatments. The cancer is out of her system."

"Oh my god!" I exclaimed happily as I watched mom and dad pull Rosalinda into a hug while the doctor just had a smile on his face as he saw the scene unfold in front of him. Rosalinda then came to sit beside me and my arm went around her shoulders, pulling her into a sideways hug.

The doctor cleared his throat, the smile never once leaving his face as he continued. "You will, however, have regular check-ups and possibly scans or x-rays. These will probably continue for several years. If you have any problems, or notice any symptoms in between your appointments, let me know as soon as possible." Dr. Patel explained.

We knew that it wouldn't end just at chemotherapy, but at least now we could breathe a sigh of relief that Rosalinda is healthy.

"Since cancer is life changing, getting back to normal may take some time. It's not uncommon for you to have days when you feel less positive or are still coping with the side effects of treatment. So try not to expect too much right away and accept that it will take time to recover." He informed Rosalinda who just nodded as she listened carefully. "I recommend that you take some positive lifestyle changes. This may include eating healthily, being physically active, and to stop smoking if you do. You may also take complementary therapy to reduce stress." We all listened carefully to what the doctor was saying. "To begin with, you will usually have regular follow-up to check your progress and to discuss any concerns that you may have. Always get in touch if you have any questions in between appointments." Rosalinda nodded with a smile on her face. "It's important to remember that advice and support is available to help you with any physical or emotional problems you have."

After Dr. Patel explained to us everything we needed to know, we stood up and he walked us out. Rosalinda surprised us when she wrapped her arms around the kind doctor.

"Thank you Dr. Patel." A small smile formed on Dr. Patel's face. Rosalinda pulled back and gave him a wide smile before we all walked out.

"Thank you, Es." Rosalinda said as we walked out to the parking lot.

"What for, sweetie?"

"You always believed in me. You always thought I was strong enough to overcome this." She explained.

"I never thought, Rosa." I told her. "I always knew, and I wasn't wrong was I?" She shook her head with a small smile and hugged me sideways.

My phone vibrated in my pocket as dad drove us back home. Collin's name lighted up the screen, but I couldn't answer.

'I can't answer, babe. Is something wrong?'

Collin took no time at all to reply. 'I need you to come to my place now.'

My heart was beating rapidly as I read the message. The urgency in his message made me believe that something was wrong. Did something happen with Collin that he didn't want to tell me over the phone?

'Is everything okay, Collin?'

A few minutes later, my phone vibrated with a new text message.

'Everything's fine, beautiful. I just miss you.'

I breathed a sigh of relief. I really thought something was wrong.

'I'll be there as soon as I can.'

"Mom, can I borrow your car?" I asked her as soon as we stepped out of dad's car.

"You can borrow mine, baby girl." Dad told me before mom could reply.

I smiled at my dad. "Thank you." I made my way to the driver's seat as they all started walking towards the front door. "Don't wait up for dinner." I called out. My mom turned around and gave me a knowing smile before she walked inside the house.

I pressed the code to Collin's penthouse and tapped my foot impatiently as I waited for the elevator to reach to its designated floor. After what seemed to be like a very long time, the elevator dinged and its doors opened. I stepped out and walked to Collin's door.

Weirdly, the door was slightly open. I could hear my heart beating out of my chest. He had never left his door open. I pushed it open all the way and walked in. The penthouse was dark with only flickering candles lighting the way.

"Collin?" I called out before my eyes went to the rose petals trail on the floor and a white card. I picked up the card and read its contents.

'Follow the trail to indefinite destiny.'

I held the card in my hand and followed the trail that was leading me to the bedroom. I pushed the door open gently and gasped as my hand covered my mouth once I saw what was in front of me.

The king sized bed was draped in white and covered in rose petals that read 'Will you marry me'. Beside the bed, there was an ice bucket with champagne and strawberries. My gaze then went to Collin who was kneeling on one knee as he held an open black velvet engagement box in his hand.

I couldn't help it as a sob racked my body. I wasn't crying because I was sad, no. I was crying because I was overjoyed.

"I never thought that I would meet someone who would become the focus of my world. I never thought that a love like this existed, but when I met you Esmeralda, all of that changed. Every day I want you more. I want to see you smile, hear you laugh, and feel your touch. I cannot live without you. You stole my heart, Esmeralda, and I want you to keep it forever. This is why we're here; I'm offering everything I will ever be to the person who owns me. Esmeralda, will you marry me?"

Tears were streaking down my face as I listened to Collin speak. I couldn't believe how lucky I was. I nodded my approval then whispered yes before I jumped into his arms and held his face in my hands. I kissed him passionately. I kissed him like I never wanted to let go. I would be content; no I would be on cloud nine if I only lived from his kisses.

Collin pulled back and held my hand in his. He slipped the diamond ring onto my finger. I looked at it with tears still pouring down my face.

"This is beautiful." The ring was classically elegant with an oval yellow diamond encircled by a single row of bead-set white diamonds. "This must have cost you a fortune."

"Nothing is too expensive when it comes to you, beautiful"

"I love you." I whispered as I reclaimed his lips in a hungry kiss. "Make love to me, Collin." I whispered as I pulled back from the kiss.

Collin didn't need to be told twice as he removed my top and threw it to the side before my pants followed as well. I unbuttoned his shirt and threw it beside my clothes before his pants joined in as well.

"You're beautiful." Collin whispered as he looked at me in nothing but my lingerie.

I blushed and wrapped my arms around his waist, wanting to feel his skin on mine. He walked us to the bed and lied down with him on top of me. His hands went behind me as he unclasped my bra and removed it. He took his time massaging my breast, taking it in his mouth, and licking it whilst sending me to ecstasy before he moved down and removed my panties. With his hand, he spread my legs wider before his head disappeared between my legs. My fingers ran through his hair as I tugged on it. Moaning, I arched my back and screamed Collin's name before I fell back on the bed wanting to catch my breath. Collin came back up and looked at me so lovingly and adoringly. I wanted to please him just like he had pleased me. This time I was the one that moved down. I grabbed the waistband of his boxers and pulled them down as I looked at him straight into his eyes. I wrapped my hand around his shaft and stroked it. Collin groaned and leaned his head back. I smiled knowing he was enjoying it then removed my hand and replaced it with my mouth.

"Oh god, Es" He groaned. "Come up, beautiful, I don't want to come just yet." He told me after a few minutes.

I moved back up and he captured his lips with mine then climbed on top of me. Sliding the condom down his shaft, he positioned himself between my legs, and in one swift move, entered me. I grabbed his butt and clawed him with my nails, wanting him deeper inside me. Collin pounded into me hard. It wasn't long until I felt myself building up to my orgasm.

"Faster, Collin, faster" I pleaded. Collin pounded into me faster and harder.

"I'm so close." My voice was breathless. "You're going to make me come."

Collin grunted. "Come for me, baby. I want to watch you come for me."

That did it for me. My vision blurred, and everything became hazy. I couldn't hear anything only the sound of my heart beating erratically out of my chest. I couldn't see anything only the stars that blurred my vision. This was a sensation that I had never felt before. It was so powerful; it felt like I had left my body and went into a different world.

"Good girl." Collin's voice brought me back to reality. I blinked twice as I looked at him. He pounded into me some more until I felt him still completely as he emptied himself inside me. He flopped down beside me and held my face to his chest.

"Shhh" He comforted.

"I love you, Collin."

"I love you too, Esmeralda."

**********Remember to vote, comment, share, recommend, add 'Trixie' to your reading list, and follow. :)

Epilogue

Three years later

"I cannot believe how eager he was for me to leave the house." I complained. "I cannot believe him. I hate him so much." I exclaimed angrily to Rosalinda as we drove back to my house. Well, Collin's as well since we're married, but I wasn't fond of him very much at that moment.

"He probably just needs some father and son time." She tried to make me feel better.

My face softened as I thought about my two year old beautiful baby boy. I loved him more than life itself. He was the air I breathed.

"No." I shook my head. "Something is up with this man, and I'm going to figure it out." my voice was firm.

Rosalinda chuckled from the passenger's seat beside me. "May the lord help you, Collin." She prayed silently.

"Yes, he's going to need that prayer." I told her as I parked the car in the driveway of our home.

Collin had bought a home right before we married. He said we needed a real family home and not a bachelor's pad. As much as I loved his penthouse, I had to agree with him. We had checked out a lot of homes whilst we were house hunting, but nothing grabbed my eye the way this house did. The moment I stepped foot inside the house, I knew I wanted it. It was a modern looking house, yet very homey. I could instantly picture myself running around my babies trying to catch them.

"Hey, Es?" Rosalinda waved her hand in front of my face.

I blinked twice and looked at her. "Mm..."

"You kind of zoned out there for a moment."

I shook my head. "Yes, sorry." I brought my key out of my purse and walked to the front door. "It's eerily quiet inside, don't you think?" I asked Rosalinda who just shrugged. "And why is it dark?" I questioned as I unlocked the door and started to walk inside. "I swear to god if he's cheating on me..." I trailed off as everyone shouted.

"Surprise!"

I watched as Collin walked towards me with a smile on his face holding Philip in his arms. "Happy birthday, beautiful" He placed a soft kiss on my lips, but I was too shocked and surprised to react to his kiss.

Everyone started hugging me and wishing me a happy birthday. Mom, dad, Benjamin, Collin's parents were all in cahoots with Collin all along. I turned and looked at Rosalinda who had a grin on her face.

"You knew?" She nodded with a laugh. "I have been going on and on about Collin, and you knew all along."

She shrugged. "Sorry. I promised I wouldn't say anything." She said before she walked away to where Benjamin was.

Those two were getting quite close with each other even though he was significantly older than her. I didn't mind though since Benjamin was a really nice guy and I thought that he and Rosalinda actually looked good together. I was very glad that Rosalinda had gotten back to normal after her treatment ended even though it was hard and took a lot of time just like the doctor had said it would. My parents and I gave her as much support, advice, and love as we could give. Collin was there for her as well and even more so Benjamin. He was very understanding and supportive when she told him that she had cancer.

"Do you like the surprise?" Collin voice brought me back from my reverie.

I looked at him through narrowed eyes. "You Mr. are in big trouble."

"Why?" He asked in a confused tone with sad eyes.

"Is that why you have been trying to get me out of the house today?" He nodded guiltily. "And the secretive phone calls?"

"I wanted to do something special for your birthday, and you didn't want anything extravagant." He said.

"Babe, spending my birthday with you and Philip would be the best birthday ever." His lips turned upwards in a smile then he leaned forward and placed a soft kiss on my lips. This time I reacted and wrapped my arms around his neck, and forgot about everyone else around us right until Phillip started giggling. I pulled back and looked at my beautiful baby boy.

"What are you laughing at, baby?" I asked him in a funny voice as I took him from Collin and held him in my arms.

Philip giggled again making my heart flutter. I loved seeing him smile and laugh. If he was happy then I was happy.

We joined everyone else at the garden where Collin had apparently prepared a table full of food.

"You did this?" I asked him amazed.

He shook his head. "Everyone came early to help."

As we sat around the table and ate the delicious food, Rosalinda started telling Collin everything we talked about during our car drive back home. I gasped as I looked at my sister who just chuckled.

"I won't tell you anything anymore." I pouted as everyone at the table just laughed, Collin included.

"I would never cheat on you, beautiful." Collin whispered in my ear. "I'm in love with you, baby, hook, line, and sinker." He kissed my cheek. "Don't you ever think like that ever again." I nodded shyly.

Once we finished eating, mom and Margaret stood up from their seat and walked inside the house. A few minutes later they came out bearing a birthday cake in their hands. Yes, the cake was that big that it needed two people to carry it. I turned to look at Collin with a smile on my face then behind me at my dad who held Phillip in his arms. We all gathered around the cake as they all started singing happy birthday while Collin wrapped his arms around me and looked at me lovingly while singing happy birthday to me as well. At that moment, I felt so loved and cherished by all of my family.

"Blow the candles." Benjamin yelled once they finished singing.

"Make a wish first." Rosalinda added.

I looked around the people that surrounded me, the people that I cared about and loved very dearly. I knew what my wish would be; I wanted to be surrounded by family always. I tucked my hair behind my ear on either side before I bent forward and blew the candles.

They all started clapping as Collin handed me the knife to cut the first piece. I ran the knife through the cake and cut a very small piece then turned around and made airplane noises. Philip giggled happily before he opened his mouth and I placed the piece of cake in his mouth. I held his face in both my hands and placed a kiss on his cheeks.

"I love you, baby boy." I told him as I kissed him again.

"Let's eat cake!" Benjamin yelled as everyone laughed.

#

"Happy birthday, Es" Margaret wished me once more as she stood at the door with Silas about to leave.

"Thank you." I said to both of them.

"This is for you." Silas handed me a black rectangular velvet box.

"Open it." Margaret urged me eagerly.

Opening the lid, I gasped at the beautiful diamond bow necklace. "This is beautiful." I looked up at both of them. "But it's too much."

"It's not too much, Esmeralda." She assured me. "You deserve more."

My lips turned upwards in a smile. "Thank you." I hugged her and sent a smile Silas's way.

My parents stood up to leave a few minutes later. Dad held a box in his hands and handed it to me. "This is for you, baby girl. Happy birthday"

I pulled my dad into a hug before hugging my mom. "You shouldn't have bought anything."

"We wanted to" My mom assured me.

This time, I didn't wait for anyone to tell me to open it as I ripped it open and gasped. "This is beautiful." I said honestly as I brought the cashmere scarf out of the box and wrapped it around my neck. "I love it. It's so cozy." My fingers smoothed the material. "Thank you." I beamed at my parents.

"You're welcome, sweetheart." They hugged me one more time before they left.

I noticed that Rosalinda didn't leave with them. I turned and looked at her with a raised eyebrow. "How come you didn't leave with mom and dad?"

Rosalinda suddenly blushed."I'm taking her home." Benjamin piped up.

"Oh, really?" I walked closer towards him. "So, you're in a relationship?" I asked as I pointed my finger between him and Rosalinda.

"You're in a relationship?" Collin asked, surprise lacing his tone.

"We're just getting to know each other." Rosalinda broke her silence.

"You do know he is significantly older than you, Rosalinda. Don't you?"

"Are you saying I'm an old man?" Benjamin put his hand on his heart in mock hurt. "I'm not that older than her."

"He really isn't." Collin whispered from beside me. I turned and looked at him as he held Philip in his arms then turned back to look at Rosalinda and Benjamin.

"I thought you'd be happy for me." Rosalinda told me disappointedly.

"Oh, I am more than happy for you, sweetie." I told her as I walked towards her and hugged her. "I'm just making sure that you know he is older than you."

Rosalinda smiled brightly. "I know."

"Now it's my turn to give you your gift." Benjamin said excitedly. I chuckled and turned around as he practically shoved a box in my face. "Open it." He eagerly said. I opened the box and my eyes widened as I looked at him then back at the box.

"Do you like it?" Rosalinda asked me. "I chose it"

"I love it!" I beamed as I brought the Chloe shoulder bag out of the box."Thank you, Ben." I beamed at him. "You too, Rosa"

Benjamin and Rosalinda hugged me and wished me a happy birthday before they walked out.

"Alone at last" Collin sighed happily as he rocked Philip on his knee.

I sat down beside him and held Philip in my arms. "I love you, baby boy."

Philip wrapped his small hands around my neck as Collin snaked his arm around my waist.

"I love you too, Collin."

"I love you more, Es."

#

"Did Philip go to sleep?" Collin asked me as I crawled under the covers and wrapped my arms around his naked torso.

"Yes."

"I've been waiting to give you your birthday present since this morning, but I held myself back." He said.

My hand went under the covers wanting my present as well when Collin's larger hand grabbed mine; stopping me. I looked up at him with a pout while Collin just chuckled.

"That is gift number two." He smirked.

"Oh." I was confused.

He opened his bedside table drawer and brought out a white envelope then handed it to me. I looked at him questioningly while he just nodded at me, urging me to open it.

My eyes widened at what was inside. This day could not get any better. "I can't believe this." I blinked at the tickets unbelievingly.

"Oh, but you have to, beautiful." He said. "You, Philip, and I are going to Hawaii."

I wrapped my arms around Collin's neck. "Thank you, handsome."

"I would like to receive my thank you in another way." He said once I pulled back from the hug.

"Your wish is my demand." I smirked at him before we spent the rest of the night making sweet, sweet love.

The End

**********Remember to vote, comment, share, recommend, add 'Trixie' to your reading list, and follow. :)

CPSIA information can be obtained
at www.ICGtesting.com
Printed in the USA
LVHW041229030123
736313LV00011B/859

9 781837 616398